Tuesday was Two Days Ago

Jerry Martinez

Tuesday was Two Days Ago
by Jerry Martinez
ISBN 978-1-7337939-3-3

Cover art by Mary Ancilla Martinez.

Published by Michael Martinez
PO Box 64324, Sunnyvale CA 94088
Printed on demand starting 09/2020

For correspondence please email jiralda@aol.com or write to the above address.

About the Cover Artist

Mary Ancilla Martinez Taasevigen is a New Mexican born artist who paints the liminal…those in between spaces…the misty and mystical, wild and free ethereal places where unseen greets seen, where dark weaves light, and land meets sea and sky. Martinez Taasevigen enjoys the exploration of dreams, mythology, archetypes, alchemy and metaphysics. She is deeply inspired by nature…secret whispers from the desert winds, the language of trees, the power and magnificence of animals, the dynamism of the elements, and the infinity of the stars and cosmos. Her work is primarily figurative and narrative, created mainly in oils. Her current focus examines personal sovereignty inspired by Greek, Celtic, Spanish, French, African and Indigenous mythology. Martinez Taasevigen strives for meaning and intention in each piece and simultaneously enjoys the engagement found in pure process. She seeks a feeling of transcendence in her paintings and desires for her work to touch the viewer with a sense of the divine.

Chapter One

Laura doesn't know why she's awake so early. No school today, yet she's up at 7:00 a.m.

She blearily searches for her glasses and stumbles to the bathroom. For some reason she looks askance (she used to think it was *ask once*) at her dresser and spies an odd-looking note written in an unfamiliar hand on very unusual luminescent paper. It seems alive, practically moving of its own accord as though it has more to convey than mere words:

"Tuesday was two days ago."

But no time to ponder it. She is starving and had best get to the kitchen before her brother eats all the cereal. Stuffs the note into her pocket, runs to the sink, yanks her glasses off, douses her face in cold water, slips the glasses back on, glances in the mirror. Whew.

She's nearly thirteen and, though a tomboy, likes to be neat. Her short curly hair stands on end. Is it because she routinely plugs her finger into an electric socket? Perhaps the hair is the result of a fright caused by a nightmare? Could all those smuggled bedtime nachos be the culprit?

Nah, her hair has been macaroni-the-color-of-tomato-sauce foreverrr.

Her mother, lifting her coffee cup, asks, "Do you have plans for the weekend?"

"Not really," she munches her cereal. Mild warmth emanates from where the note is in her pocket, but she's busy with thoughts of trees, marble shoots, and a search for apples for the neighbor's horse, her equine friend for years.

"Well, don't forget your regular chores," her mother admonishes.

Smile. Burp. She rushes back upstairs to brush her teeth. As she speeds past her dresser she remembers the note. Where the dickens did it come from?? As if on cue, her pocket vibrates gently. How odd. With tremulous breath and mounting nervousness she slowly removes the scrap of paper.

1

This is freaking her out. Again she reads the missive:

"Tuesday was two days ago."

Tuesday was not two days ago! It was more like four days ago. Not that she's good at arithmetic. Let's see. Tuesday to Saturday is four days, right? Not three, not five?

Certainly not *two*! Oh, brother. This reminds her of the puzzle she was going to write for Crusty Ole Chip, the math and science teacher:

You are next to the bay door in the cargo hold of a military jet as it prepares to land. You're standing in a giant spoon, the bottom of which you have greased and the handle of which you have outfitted with a bridle. The jet descends to the runway, doing about 200 mph as it touches down. Helmet on, reins firmly gripped in one hand, you press the button to open the cargo door, push off and zoom out. Harder to maneuver than you'd imagined, you hafta lean left then right so as not to be un-spooned. The hypothesis is that you leave the plane at 20mph.

Question 1: how far away from the receding plane, if it takes a quarter mile to come to a halt, will you be when you stop? Feel free to throw in some velocity figures, wind factors, things that impress the teacher, and show your work.

Question 2 (the most important): will you survive the experiment?

Her musings are halted by a barely audible hum emanating from the note. She ponders the Tuesday thing again, which reminds her of Einstein who had come up with an *m=something squared* thingy about time and space. At this point, the paper in her hand almost crackles with excitement.

She'll have to talk to her best friend about it. Justin lives a couple blocks down the street. They'd known one another since they were chubby toddlers unsteady on their feet. Their friendship had been cemented with giggles, tumbles and bops with toys on the head.

Laura figures he's home as his bike is on the porch but when she calls his name as she goes through the door, she's met with tangible silence. Uh-oh. Quietly checks behind the sofa and chairs. No one there. Glances through the kitchen then carefully and with bated breath tiptoes to the hall.

This game could be nerve-wracking. Slithers down to the floor and creeps along inch by wormy inch. Hmm. There are a couple of large boxes at the end of the hall. Better not let them distract. The bedroom doors are all closed. Not good! Dare open a door? No, keep going but watch your flank. Cautious approach to a black-marked sign on cardboard, "Herein lies a puzzle of great import." Wonder....eeek!! Even as she turns and her brain screams May Day! May Day!, she's slammed from the side. Oof. Good one but she hasn't cried uncle yet. Flipping over, she scissors her legs around Justin and tries to grapple his arms. They struggle until suddenly he flushes, shouts stop.

"Crying uncle so soon?" she taunts. He is extremely red and refuses to look at her. She immediately releases him. "Justin?"

"I gotta go."

He's behaved strangely the last few weeks. She cannot figure him out. Wonders if he's in some kind of trouble but he refuses to discuss it.

Soooooo, before he makes it to the door, she reaches for the note and hands it over. Intrigued, he agrees it might have to do with time travel. He drops it when it warms to the point of being uncomfortable. They stare as a bit of smoke wafts from the rug. He stomps on it to no avail.

"Quick, there's an empty box on the book shelf in my room."

They strong-arm the agitated note into the metal box and, panting, slam the lid.

"Did you notice?"

"What?"

"It didn't tear. It's paper, but it didn't tear. Didn't burn, either."

"Not real paper? We should run tests."

"What kind of tests?"

"I dunno if we could ask Ms. Chip about something like this. What would a science teacher think - that she was in the Land of Oz?"

Giggling, they put the box in a corner of the closet where his mom refuses to clean.

Tense from the encounter and hungry, their attention turns to ice cream followed by tree climbing, chewing stalks of grass underneath the willow tree, marbles, feeding oats to the horse owned by their neighbor, Old Robert.

Back at school a couple days later, the Justin puzzle is beginning to preoccupy her thoughts on a disturbingly daily basis.

****

There were subtle differences in Justin's behavior those last weeks before summer vacation. They still frequently got together to bike around the neighborhood, read books in the tree house, the usual stuff, but they'd never again played the stealth game. She brought it up a couple of times since it was so much fun, but the confusing so-and-so waved it off, seemingly nonchalant.

Her mom notices her preoccupation and asks what's on her mind. Almost whining, she says she doesn't understand Justin anymore. He sometimes studies her in a withdrawn manner, emotions hidden. There's an intermittent raspy quality to his voice she's learned not to laugh at or mimic. For sure he doesn't spend as much time with her as before. What truly exasperates her are the girls, flighty as birds, who flock (yes, flock) to him. His bewilderment only intrigues the little vipers.

Silly birds or vipers? Why not both? A flock of flapping vipers, har-har.

Her mom, happy to launch into her danged wise-as-an-owl lecture voice, says Justin is becoming an adult. As horrified as if she'd heard he'd been diagnosed with an incurable disease, she gapes, a fish out of water.

"What?!" she screeches. "Why? What am I going to do?!"

"There's nothing you can do." Her mom hugs her. "It's inevitable, and I hate to point out that it's going to happen to you, too. But, you know what? You can still play. You'll always be able to play, just in a bigger body." She loves her mom but rolls her eyes anyway.

Laura resigns herself as best she can to semi-losing the friend of her life. She reads even more that summer and takes ballet back-to-back with a martial arts class. She likes them equally. The ballet for its beauty as well as discipline. The martial arts also for its discipline - but mostly because it's kick-ass.

The hurt, lodged deep in her chest, at times choking her, begins to dissipate but doesn't go away completely.

Good thing her activities take a great deal of her time because Justin starts high school that fall which means they won't walk to school or have lunch together. Her life goes from weird to weirder.

****

Eighth grade might not be too bad. She will have to wade through math and science classes, subjects that will continue to plague her through high school and beyond. On the positive side, English Lit, creative writing and art will be there to lift her from the class morass.

Her first course is, groan, math. She briefly glances around the classroom to look for any excuse to avoid doing the problems. One time she had "accidentally" stumbled out of the classroom under pretext of momentary discombobulation, but the teacher became wise and now the door was blocked by the unwavering stance of the no-longer-gullible Crusty Ole Chip.

What to do to make it through the hour? Starts off with a far-away expression as if deep in mathematical thought. Pensively she twirls a lock of hair as though aloofly counting each strand. Doodles with the occasional heavily blackened number to throw off any cursory teacher observation. She manages to use up five whole-number minutes.

More interminable time passes.

Her eyes alight on the girl next to her who seems to be dispatching the problems with panache, face radiant with each joyous flick of the wrist.

5

Yikes, she's in Hades.

The math whiz leans over to ask to borrow an eraser. She needs to make a correction?! There's a god after all!

Nooo, it's not for any corrections. The girl rewrites her name in calligraphy and attempts to draw flowers and vines. Well, at least the drawings are horrible. Despite that straight black hair, she isn't perfect.

Sigh, back to the problems. Time drags on but the bell finally rings. Black Beauty turns to give her the eraser and holds out her hand. "I'm Mythril. Thanks for the save."

"Huh?"

Mythril frowns. "You saved me from boredom. Drawing is a real challenge. It keeps my brain occupied. You know, all that design stuff, three-dimensional crap, negative and positive space, light source. It drives me batty."

"Exactly like math and science for me!" Laura huffs.

"Not for me. Math and science are my two loves. Maybe we can help each other out. I noticed your doodles kept you from doing the problems."

"Uh, yeah." Laura stares. "Sure. We could meet up after school. By the way, I'm Laura."

"Sure, Red. See ya!"

Chapter Two

Mythril, of all things. How did a math and science whiz kid end up with such a cool name?

It turns out she was as cool as her name, though over the next several lunch breaks it taxed Laura's brain when she started spouting off stuff about the Mossbauer effect, Heisenberg's law of physics, Einstein's theory of relativity, blah, blah. Good thing she could concentrate on slurping her milk shake between such info bites. Gamma rays, atomic nuclei bound in solids, the uncertainty principle, how the act of observing a thing changes it (what?), deja vu and Schrödinger's cat. Harrumph.

More like fantasy. Which reminds her of something. Wait a minute, wait just one skinny minute…

"Tuesday was two days ago," she shouts triumphantly.

Mythril chokes on her shake as everyone else in the ice cream shop glares.

Laura is too hyped to care. "There's this magic note that appeared out of nowhere on my dresser one morning. I didn't recognize the handwriting. The paper it was written on was luminescent." She lowers her voice. "It was as if it were alive, almost moving on its own."

Mythril holds up her hand. "That's not possible."

"For reals! It hummed! It crackled! Then I was reminded of Einstein because Tuesday definitely wasn't two days ago!"

"Of course not," Mythril states, "because today is Tuesday."

"No, no, you don't understand. The note says Tuesday was two days ago. But it wasn't! At least not when it appeared on my dresser. It was more like four or five days ago. The day I read the note, Tuesday was several days prior.   Look, I took it to Justin."

"Who's Justin?"

"My best friend ever. Er, he used to be but something happened. He changed. Look, I don't know quite what happened. Anyway, I took the note to Justin who also ended up thinking it very strange and agreed it might have to do with time travel. When he said this, the note heated up, a lot, but it didn't burn. Freaked us out, I'll tell you. We wrestled it into a box and put it in his closet. It's still there since Justin and I have sort of drifted apart." She looks down as her eyes fill with tears. She wouldn't cry, she wouldn't, not in front of all these people.

Mythril reaches over to pat her hand. "Okay, let's think about this. Approach it as the scientific problem it is."

"You mean conundrum," Laura grins.

"Conundrum, problem, it's all the same."

"Not quite. Problem is, well, a more straightforward word. You mean we are looking for a solution to a scientific problem. Conundrum is a bit trickier, no solution, i.e., no scientific solution. The latter is what we're dealing with."

Mythril stares. "Feel free to help me with English. In any case, you'll have to convince me. I'm a very skeptical person."

"You're on. There's one, uh, problem. I'm sure Justin still has the note; he would never get rid of it. But since we're no longer close…" she looks at the table, blinking, "it feels awkward to approach him."

Mythril considers. "Okay. Let's start with research, then. Remember, I need to approach it from a scientific perspective. Maybe, maybe it has to do with, there's something called ods, a hypothetical force thought at one time to pervade all nature, to manifest itself in magnetism, mesmerism, chemical action, and so forth. As soon as I read mesmerism – animal magnetism, really?! - I dismissed the whole thing. However, could you have somehow been hypnotized?"

"What are the ods?" quips Laura.

Mythril throws her napkin at her.

Laura rolls her eyes. They burst into laughter.

Pointing her ice cream laden spoon at Mythril, "So you'll entertain the idea of hypnotism but not mesmerism even though they both end in ism."

Mythril boos. "There are other ism words, schism, for instance." Frustrated, "Why do I let myself be drawn into word for the sake of word discussions?"

"I heard somewhere that in mathematics you can prove an elephant can fly. Is that a fable?" Laura distracts her. "Dumbo does have extraordinarily large ears."

"You're crazy. Pass the salt."

"Such a conundrum." Snort. "Anyway, when my mind wandered to time travel and Einstein's theory of relativity – I do have a thimble of scientific knowledge - the note vibrated as though I was on the right track. So, could Cronos have anything to do with this?"

Mythril frowns. "Cronos?"

"Surely you've heard of Cronos, the Greek god of time? Or was he a Titan? Ravager of time? Father Time, the fellow with the harvest scythe, the guy who purportedly ate his children." Musing. "He the past, his children the future. He thought they were going to do him in. Boy, not much has changed. Look at royalty, modern dictators. Okay, never mind, back to the past. Chronological, linear, as opposed to the right moment for something to happen…more than confusing, all the layers added by emerging temporal societies. Oh, I think the Romans ended up calling him Saturn. We need to research this to be as accurate as possible with all the convolutions."

"Porpoisely ate his children? I can't believe I just said that. Could we please stick to facts? We're scientific investigators, not fantastical faeries or speculative Neanderthals." Waves her hand dismissively. "Oh, gawd, I have to launder my brain."

"Porpoisely? Speculative Neanderthals? Now you're cooking. But you have to admit Einstein, one of the greatest scientists of all time, theorized about time travel. The only reason I remember anything about it is the phrase curvature of time and space. Caught my artistic attention. Ended up painting an abstract of imagined planets and the cosmos set in a curved time line."

"What? And can you quit with the puns already! My ribs hurt." Takes a bite of her ribs, i.e. (mentally mimicking her cohort), those on her plate.

Laura smiles excitedly, "Just imagine this hilarious scene: we somehow learn to time travel, albeit in a careening way, pick up Einstein on our journey to seek Cronos. Einstein faints when he sees His Godliness or His Titaniness or His Whatever in all his mythological majesty."

Before she can finish her thought, Mythril interrupts. "Why would we look for Cronos?!"

"You call yourself a scientist? Doesn't that mean you set about trying to prove or disprove theories? Where's your bloodhound nose? I know you haven't seen the note, but it exists!!" Laura continues. "Look, way back in history one clever cave man discovered how to hit his obnoxious neighbor using a handy club and then later, probably this same low-brow, skin-clad entrepreneur, a really distant ancestor to those Wall Street guys, came up with the idea of the wheel. The wheel, think of it. Isn't that amazing?"

"Wall Street Neanderthals? Slow down. You're hyperventilating. I'll call over Buck Teeth cause I'm not giving you mouth to mouth."

"Buck Teeth? That's cruel." They turn to look at the cute nerd across the room who hurriedly averts his gaze.

"Had to get your attention somehow," Mythril justifies her remarks in a fumbling way. Hmm, is there a blossoming romance between her best friend and this mystery guy? This bears some thought.

"I can't slow down. The words have to exit…Wall Street Neanderthals, ha. Finally, we're connecting." Mythril looks alarmed. "Where was I? Oh, at some point these cave types - not to be prejudiced - after they could string together and understand more than a grunt or two, began to wonder about the world around them. The sun, the moon, the seasons. Wow, basically the clockwork of the universe. They noticed the behavior of birds and animals, migratory patterns. Goodness, they began to plan their hunts." Pauses, a sad expression sweeps over her face. "Think of the terrors of lightning, wild fires, poisonous plants, drowning, disease, which they could not explain, the poor dears." Looks at the scene outside the window. "They started telling stories around cozy fires, their primitive language supplemented with hand gestures, awkward drawings in dirt using sticks, actual facial expressions since no one had Botox, to account for all these mystifying phenomena." Her words tumble like gurgling water over stones. "The beliefs and myths could be harebrained, but what if some small part of them was true? C'mon."

"Fine, you're right, of course, about the prove/disprove method."

"Thank you. Gee whiz."

"One caveat, I'll really enjoy kicking these theories to the curb."

The bell rings. "When can we meet again? Can you come to my house this weekend? Wait, you know the word caveat?" Mythril swats her.

They settle on two weekends into the future and part still chattering and giggling excitedly.

****

Laura answers the summons when Mythril rings the doorbell. "Hey, this is Mythril. Mythril, these are my parents, Samantha and David, otherwise mom and dad." Smiles and handshakes all around.

"There are pizza, cookies, drinks in the kitchen. Better get there before Matt eats it all."

They rush to the kitchen. "This is my brother, Matt. Matt, this is Mythril. Careful, she's a math and science whiz."

"Oh?" about to bite into a cookie. "Bet I can beat you in chess."

"We'll see about that," Mythril challenges, grabbing a slice of pizza. Her eyes widen.

"Mom makes everything from scratch," smirks Matt. "Not that she milks a cow, though we do have a few chickens and a kitchen garden and fruit trees."

Unfortunately for the note, they had to deal with art and math homework instead.

In her room, Laura talks about modeling to show volume on paper. She makes a series of broad charcoal marks on newsprint, increasing the pressure of each stroke to demonstrate light to dark. She places a roll of toilet tissue and a roll of white paper towels on the art table, one to the side and slightly behind the other. She elaborates a bit on negative and positive space and how her brain tends to zero in on negative space which at times works against her. She makes a quick thumbnail sketch, the preliminary equivalent of an outline of the drawing. It grabs the essential shapes and illustrates spatial relationship.

After toiling a good while, Mythril huffs in frustration. "Everything you said is logical. For instance, squint occasionally to more easily see the variations of light and shadow, hold your pencil at arm's length to nail the breadth and width, but my roll of toilet paper and paper towels look like pigs in a blanket. Aarrgh."

"It takes practice. Lots and lots of practice. Hundreds and thousands of drawings," Laura says. Depressively, thinks Mythril. "Take more time to look at the objects, follow the outline of the shapes with your eyes." Several minutes pass. "Pancakes and sausages, huh? Time for a food break." In such a rush, they crash into each other at the top of the stairs.

Back in her room, Laura begs Mythril to slow down with the algebra; it's too fractious. They tediously review the problems until she finally exhibits a glimmer of understanding. Mythril gives her time to work independently, but an hour later she has to be drilled again. By this time she has a headache. "Can we have a snack? A movie would be beneficial." They gallop downstairs.

Chapter Three

Monday morning Laura waves tentatively at Justin when they spy each other across the intersection. He smiles and waves back. She doesn't notice he stops to watch as she continues in the opposite direction. When she sees him again a couple weeks later, she assumes he's working on some extracurricular project. Their schools have slightly different schedules and they've never bumped into one another en route. She smiles enthusiastically, happy she feels less tense, happy he seems less awkward.

Thereafter, they wave and occasionally cross the street for a quick chat. Not as easy with one another as before, nonetheless, it lightens her aspect, gives an extra bounce to her naturally bubbly step. Of course, Mythril notices and comments. "Oh, nothing," Laura throws a hand into the air, not ready to talk, afraid she'll jinx herself. Mythril narrows her eyes, "I'll find out, you know."

Laura's mother also notices her lightheartedness but refrains from saying anything.

****

By the time Thanksgiving arrives, Laura has met Mythril's parents, Sunflower and Travis. Sunflower's real name is Ann; her parents gave her the nickname due to her happy disposition. Beads, sandals and swishy skirts, that's Sunflower. She fashions sea glass and crystal jewelry to sell in boutiques and art and craft shows. Travis, an established writer, sells articles on botany and the natural world in between espionage novels and mysteries.

"How in the world did you end up a math and science nerd?"

"Oh, a mischievous fairy bestowed these gifts on me when I was born in our castle, several centuries ago."

"No way."

****

The note languishes in its box atop Justin's closet shelf while November eases into December and Christmas seriously picks up its cue.

"Now here's a relatively modern myth perpetrated by adults on their gullible children. Poor wee ones believe some jolly guy flies through the air in a sleigh drawn by reindeer to deliver presents on Christmas eve, millions of presents in one night! There are different ideas about how this started. Santa Claus nee St. Nick back in the day bestowed gold on three maidens too poor to have dowries to attract husbands."

Mythril, shocked. "That's sick."

"You begrudge their gold bounty?"

"No. They needed money to obtain husbands?"

"Where the heck have you been? Didn't you take history classes? Read novels? You're like seriously gapped in your education."

"Gapped in my education. Gapped. You should talk about a lack of education. It's not a verb."

"Wanna bet?"

Backtracking. "If it is a verb, you didn't use it properly in the context of whatever you said." Mythril rubs her forehead.

"It's called license. What did you do in history class?"

"Endeavored to look attentive. I held the textbook up while working calculus problems. Loved my extracurricular math."

"How did you pass?"

Diverting. "What are the other stories about the origin of Santa Claus?"

Laura gasps. "Did you cheat?"

Talk about happy diversions, the bell rings.

****

"I'll tell you about it sometime," blushes Mythril in the cafeteria the next day, referring to her lopsided education. "Don't Christmas and winter solstice enjoy a correlation of some kind?"

Amazed, Laura says, "What would you know about winter solstice?"

"They're really close on the calendar. I do hear snippets of conversation. I have parents, you know."

"I thought you hatched from aliens and the nice couple I met at your house adopted you out of pity."

"I thought a pelican dropped you down the chimney, pre-diapered."

They grin.

"If you were born to humans, you must've been born with a calculator."

"No, I was born with data spewing from my mouth instead of the normal squalling. Whereas, you breathed dragon fire and set the bedding aflame, so you're the hatchling."

They take a break from banter to finish lunch.

****

Finally, Christmas, ah, winter break. The doorbell chimes. Expecting Mythril, Laura is shocked to see Justin, his hands behind his back. "Hi," he smiles hesitantly. "Hi." "Uh." "Oh, would you like to come in?" Lame. They used to pop back and forth any old time.

Her mom comes in as they sit on the sofa. "Justin! How nice. How have you been? I've really missed you." Hugs him hard. "Would you like cookies and hot chocolate?" He nods, a lump in his throat.

One hand is still hidden from view. Suddenly, he remembers. "I brought you something for Christmas." "You did?" "Yes." "I got you something, too." His eyes crinkle.

"Do you wanna open them now? Cause I'm spending this Christmas with my grandparents."

"Be right back," as she jumps up. Mortified, she almost trips on the stairs in her haste.

They smile at each other, at nothing, at each other again, munching oatmeal cookies and drinking hot chocolate. Then they carefully throw the gifts, crisscrossing, up in the air before sedately unwrapping them, just like they used to do. He's given her a gold and garnet dragon and a pi symbol on a neck chain. "Pi?" one eyebrow rises. "It's for luck in math class. And I've always thought of you as a fiery if petite dragon." She bites a grin into submission. "A book on black and white photography. Wow. How did you know?" "I remember you enthused about a show you'd gone to once. I hope you like it." He stares at her, eyes warm, before "Enthused. Only you."

Awkward again, he gets up to leave. "I'll see you around." "Sure." A sort of jig before hugging. She escorts him to the porch. Small waves.

She has the most tantalizing dreams that night. Holy cow, as her mom would say.

The holiday aftermath is subdued as she wonders, *What does it all mean?* Her heart develops an extra chamber solely for contemplation and dreams. Too quickly it's back to school, she and Justin reduced to the rare opportunity of waving at the intersection.

****

"You know, when we pick up Einstein on our way to see Old Cronie Boy, we should stop in Ireland, say, 900 A.D. Think of Einstein's expression when he meets a mage by the name of Eis McSquard." Doubles over with laughter.

Mythril finishes chomping a carrot. "Your imagination gets wilder and wilder. And how did you come across Eis McSquard?"

"I vaguely remember his name somewhere. And it would, oh, loosen Einstein up for meeting Cronos. Uh, do you think these characters could be dangerous?"

"I'd be more concerned for their welfare, facing off with you. You'll confound them with your peculiar logic. No, not logic. Bite me, your

16

particular brain. Peculiar brain. Do you ever shine a light in there to rid it of cobwebs and mold?" Dodges Laura's bread stick. "You are entertaining. I'll give you that. Plus useful in art and English. Amazing in those subjects, actually."

"Back atcha. Thanks for your efforts to help in math. I got a D- on the last test. Teach almost fainted with pleasure. She took me aside to suggest a class party but that would've been embarrassing. She ended up saying she hopes I continue the good work and gave me a math joke book! Want it? It's all-out Greek to me."

"Sure, for a relaxing bedtime read. Hey, I read somewhere, perhaps an Oriental proverb, about how two days from now, tomorrow will be yesterday."

Laura's impressed eyebrows disappear into her hairline. "Quite the philosopher, there."

"Have to admit this type of thought process is interesting, if disturbing. Leads to what ifs, how fors, correction, how evers, nevers."

"Terrible non-words, but I get your drift, I think."

Mythril, brooding. "Heisenberg law of physics, uncertainty principle, a thing or the very act of observing it changes it." Laura gripes, 'We're back to this?" Mythril, undeterred, "Deja vu and Schrödinger's cat – is the cat dead or not?"

"Now who's spouting fantasy and sci-fi?! You've been holding out. And that's beyond creepy. Is the cat dead or not!"

Mythril continues to muse. "Nano-technology, additive manufacturing or AM, 3d printing."

"You're not making sense."

"If time travel is possible, I wonder what practical applications there would be. Time advance, for instance, three hours advanced on Monday to allow you to go to court to pay that traffic ticket before work. Might shorten your lifespan if you don't repay by the end of the month when time interest begins to accumulate. Would there be time interest? Of course, hmm, time bankers, the little weasels."

"How should I know?"

"The ripple effects, cross time currents, could be scary. My preliminary conclusion is that time travel is not possible. It's quite illogical, messing with the natural order of things. If it is possible, it's certainly not feasible."

"Maybe it's magical."

"My intuition says not possible, magically, if there's such a thing, or scientifically."

"Aha, intuition. Define intuition," Laura taunts.

"Define magic."

Back and forth they go through the end of eighth grade, past summer and slam dunk into the new school year.

Chapter Four

She rounds the corner at speed. Wham! Her glasses fly off. Hands reach out to steady her. A timbered voice says, "Take it easy." She gropes the blur. Really, contact lens might be worth the effort.

"Lexicon and obelisk," she mutters.

"What?"

"So sorry."

The fuzzy blob in front of her chuckles, "It's okay."

They bend to search for the frigging things and classically bump heads.

"Wait, here they are. Uh-oh, they snapped in two. Why don't I walk you to the nurses's office."

One warm hand reaches for hers, the other gently touches her back.

"Thanksgiving."

"Should I be disturbed I understand you?"

Holding one lens up, she looks at her blur. Surprise flows over her, sets her off, "'Prise. Purple pleasure. Painful. Platitude. Burp."

He laughs low, "Burp?"

"The p's at the end."

"And 'prise?"

"Your voice is…different. We haven't talked in quite a while."

"That'll change," under his breath. "I'm sorry. It's my fault. There are things we need to discuss. Meanwhile, I'll walk you to the nurse's office. You know, you always did love unstrung words."

"Yes," she sighs happily. "They're like beads ready to be put together. For instance, you could end up with 'The feat of the fete rested solely on feet,' whatever that means. Mayhap it has to do with dancing."

19

****

Laura timidly enters the sex education classroom early so she can take a seat in the back. She doesn't look up till someone sits next to her. Oh, gawd, it's Justin! "I waited till we could take the class together," he says. Her complexion merges with her red hair, her eyes round. She mouths a silent oh.

"Yes," he whispers. "I don't want things to continue as they have. I backed away from you last year because I, uh, began to have a different type of feeling for you. It was confusing as all heck. I had no clue as to how to behave. Then your dad noticed and took me aside to have a discussion about the birds and the bees."

"The birds and the bees."

"Well, yeah, you know. He was very natural about the whole subject, talked as if I were an adult which made it easier but, still… He's always treated me like a son." Eyes moisten. "He was very sensitive. Told me to be open with you when the time came but advised I wait till my intuition kicks in and smacks me on the head posthaste. That's the way he put it." Smiles at the memory.

Laura gulps. "You're talking about…"

He cups her face with gentle hands and blurts out the name of the elephant in the room, "Sex."

She stares, the information crammed into the last few moments tumbling in her brain like clothes in a dryer. Then her face splits into the widest grin she's ever had. Relieved, he asks, "Are we good?" She nods vigorously, "My mom had the same talk with me a few months ago. Birds and bees, indeed."

The first class touches briefly in a dry clinical manner on the physical aspects of the mating ritual, as the teacher calls it. The rest of the time he concentrates on respect and responsibility for oneself and others, protection, thoughtfulness. Justin leans over, "Thoughtful? Elegantly formal? Care for sugar and milk with your tea?" They collapse against each other.

****

Laura and Justin are seated at lunch in the cafeteria. A couple of boys saunter over. Their good looks cheapened by the smug expressions on their faces. The tall auburn haired guy says, "Hey, Laura, I've been noticing you. You're actually pretty hot. How about meeting up after school?"

Laura flushes, staring at her leek soup. Justin frowns. Is she affected, flattered, in any way by this douche bag? It takes a moment for her composure to return. She looks at him, pleading.

He knows her like the back of his hand, so why the doubt? Ahh, jealousy had never gripped him before, but that's because no one had moved in on his Laura.

He takes a deep breath and scoots closer to drape an arm over her shoulders, to take her hand and bring it to his lips for a tender kiss. She gawks, searching his face. Her gaze falls on his lips. They curl in a lopsided grin, dimples framing their sensitivity. Boy, is his mouth ever attractive. It takes but a second for him to lean in, muttering roughly at the idiot, "She's with me," before kissing her. On the mouth.

They don't notice when the two slouches turn away.

Justin smiles against her mouth, "Glad that's been cleared up." She sighs and snuggles closer, if possible. "Yeah."

A few moments later, Mythril comes bounding up, crosses her arms and demands, "What's this I hear about a kiss?" Justin looks up from Laura, "You mean the kiss." Mythril casts her eyes at the ceiling, "Duh. You were the only ones who didn't seem to know what was going on between you."

"I've known forever," says Justin. He and Mythril turn to Laura whose face is as red as her hair, "I, um, well, I was hoping…that is, I've known forever, too," defensively.

Happy as three musketeers, they head off for class.

****

Justin's heart is light, its heavy load released into the atmosphere like a helium balloon. Laura and he are back on a comfortable footing. No, it's more than that. Gushing, yes, a gushing tumultuous sensation that somehow goes hand in hand with comfortable, like a swift river on a peaceful day. *I know we are very young, but I also know to my very core, we will be together for eternity.* He smiles when Buzz Lightyear pops into his head. *Hey, Buzz, to infinity and beyond.*

Still, he aches for the time lost without her daily presence this last year or more. *I'm such an idiot. Maybe I could've handled it differently.* He'd done it for her sake, though, not wanting to frighten her.

Just as her father advised, it had been wise to put the brakes on. His chest hurt. He owed the guy, his surrogate father or at least that's how he views him, a big, fat hug, and he's man enough to do it.

All things come in time, after all, which reminds him of the Tuesday note squirreled away in his closet. He had taken it out a few times since Laura entrusted it to him. It hadn't seemed agitated; in fact, it was quite tame compared to it practically incinerating everything when he first handled it. Could it have something to do with his relationship with Laura?

He ran up her steps that very evening, her father giving him a high five when he opened the door, so happy to see him. David, "Everything good?" "Yep, more than good." "There's no one else for her, or you," David goes on with a huge smile, tears in his eyes, "I have all the confidence and respect in the world for you." Justin smiles broadly, "Thank you, sir." "You know, you may as well call me dad," as they hug.

Laura skips down the stairs, pinches her lips together to keep from bawling at the sight of them before she and Justin head for the kitchen where they dig into the supercalifragilistic lasagna and an afterthought salad.

****

"You know," Laura says in her room, "we need to loop you into the Tuesday note discussions Mythril and I have going. Your intellectual input would add another perspective to the whole problem, I mean conundrum."

"Conundrum, huh?" Ponders. "When did you meet Mythril?"

22

"We met in eighth grade and instantly became friends."

"Alright, cool. I did open the box a few times over the past year," clears his throat which draws Laura's attention to his jaw, er, collar, "and the note behaved, well, peacefully. I wonder if it has something to do with us as well as time travel."

"Why would it be concerned with us?" Laura asks doubtfully.

"Maybe it gave us time to mature? Before slamming us with some horrible quest."

"True." They mull over this possible aspect. "We're not exactly super heroes. What if it's the apocalypse."

"Doomsayer," he smirks.

He stills when she sticks her tongue out at him. She, in turn, looks at his mouth. Oops.

A bit later, they're back on track. "There's this theory called The Butterfly Effect, with a movie by the same name, a chaos theory about how something as subtle as the flap of a butterfly wing in one part of the world could cause a humongous storm in a completely different region. And a wild conjecture using this in time travel."

Laura frowns. Justin reaches over with a to-and-fro motion of his thumb to smooth between her eyebrows. "Don't worry. We'll figure it out. The note is on our side."

He goes on, "The Butterfly Effect has some root in physics – small changes can result in different outcomes. NASA applies it to trajectories in the solar system. But human time travel is a bit farfetched."

"Unless it's magic. Do you think magic exists? Or did at one time?" Laura coughs at the word.

"I've always tended to scoff, but the note makes me wonder. After all, we don't know everything, do we?"

"I know one thing," she says, ruffling his dark hair.

****

A girl wearing tight clothes and too much make-up approaches their cafeteria table the next day. "Is it true?" she asks Justin, deliberately ignoring Laura. "What?" he asks, irritated. "You kissed this?"

"Of course. She's not only beautiful, she has an excellent brain, and we've been friends forever. This is forever," drapes his arm around Laura and kisses the top of her head. Turns back to the skank. "Stop harassing me. Be careful what you say and do."   "Or do you want the principal to bring your parents in for a chat?"

The sleaze glares before she walks away.

Laura hugs him tight, the incident of no real consequence. They resume their discussion with Mythril who appears somewhat distracted, her attention at times riveted across the room. Laura waits till Mythril becomes engrossed with their favorite topic, expounding now on horologists.

Surreptitiously, Laura looks across the cafeteria to see a nice-looking guy seated by himself. He wears glasses and braces and casts occasional glances at Mythril. Laura suddenly remembers Buck Teeth. Ahh, he's nothing like the moniker her sly friend had used. She excuses herself from the table and walks over. "Why don't you join us for lunch?" smiling. "S-s-sure." He grabs his tray to follow.

Mythril throws Laura a trapped look when he sits next to her. Laura grins wickedly. "Sorry, I didn't introduce myself. I'm Laura. This is my boyfriend, Justin," grins broadly at the DTR.   "And this is our friend, Mythril."

"I'm W-wolf," the newcomer says bashfully. Justin reaches over to shake his hand. "Glad to meet you." Mythril turns, "Me, too." There's an audible electric shock when they clasp hands. Conversation briefly halts.

Justin, "We're discussing the possibility of time travel."

Wolf, still caught up in Mythril's beautiful blue eyes, finally engages his brain. "Why time travel?" A calm eliminates his stutter after their initial encounter.

The three friends exchange looks, come to a silent agreement.

"You see," Justin confides in a low voice, "Laura happened across a very interesting note."

They interrupt each other to put forth their own ideas as they hasten to bring him up to speed. Overwhelmed, Wolf whistles low before he launches into his first quip, "'Time is of the essence,'" followed by the ancient proverb, "'Time and tide wait for no man,'" attributed to Saint Marher in the year 1225. It's actually, "'And te tide and te time pat tu iboren were, schal beon iblescet.'"

They stare at Wolf before whooping in exhilaration.

"Ancient history and language are my favorite subjects."

"Why, you're like our fourth dimension," exclaims Laura.

"Time and space," murmurs Mythril.

The infernal bell rings. "Let's get together after school," they chorus.

Chapter Five

They grab seats in the public library, "We can theorize till the moon comes home," says Justin.

"You mean the cows come home," guffaws Laura, patting him on the head.

Justin smiles. "Just seeing if you were paying attention," he whispers in her ear. "Always," she pins him with a look.

Justin turns to Mythril and Wolf, "Before our theories get completely out of hand, you need to meet the note." Mythril and Wolf, suddenly serious, glance at each other. Justin suggests, "Let's get together at my house. Saturday noon good for everyone?" Yes, yes,yes.

Mythril looks worried as Wolf walks her out of the building. "You okay?" he asks. She clears her throat. "Think I'm nervous because after all the discussions we've had, it almost became, oh, more like a fantasy sci-fi movie project than something real, though I do believe Laura's description of the note and how it behaved. Now that we're meeting it… What if we can't dismiss it as some sort of hoax? It's pretty scary."

Wolf stops and takes her hand, "We can't ignore it, either, so we'll face it head-on." Mythril takes a shuddering breath, squeezes his hand, "Alright."

****

The big day arrives. Not as big a day as the lunar landing but who knows. The four of them experience some degree of nervousness. To ease the palpably atmospheric tension, Justin takes them to the kitchen where his mom is taking a roast out of the oven before slipping in a very chocolate cake. There's homemade bread cooling on the counter. The smells are overwhelming.

"Hey, mom. This is Mythril and this is Wolf. Guys, this is my mom, Elizabeth."

"Mum" is as warm as her oven. She embraces each in turn, grinning extra wide at Laura. "The table's set. Go ahead and start." Quick as two shakes of a lamb's tail, they comply. Elizabeth bustles around before she joins them. She lost her husband, Buddy, when Justin was a boy of three but managed to be a stay-at-home mom on the life insurance and a part-time job editing.

The conversation is lively and touches on every topic but the note. Elizabeth doesn't know of its existence; they'd decided they weren't ready to mention it to their parents.

By the time they go to Justin's room and face the closet, they aren't completely apprehensive. Still, their eyes rivet on the box when he brings it down. They gulp as he slowly takes off the lid.

A second passes, two, three.

The note flies out to attach itself to Mythril's forehead. Wolf catches her as she faints, pale veins vaguely resemble crosses over her eyelids just like in cartoons.

Mythril is whiter than normal. Wolf matches her lack of color, almost on the verge of a faint himself. He rallies to pat her face. "Mythril, Mythril," quietly. He glares at the doggone note still stuck to her forehead. From the faint humming sound and nearly invisible swirl of color, it seems to be busy transmitting data but takes a second to convey a positive thought his way. He relaxes, pulls Mythril onto his lap. She's still out but is breathing.

Laura and Justin sigh with relief.

Moments later, the note peels itself off Mythril's forehead, bows and retreats to the box. Mythril stirs, eyelids fluttering. Looks up at Wolf, disoriented. "What happened?" "Shh, you're fine. We're all fine. The note attached itself to you like an octopus to a barnacle." "That's a terrible analogy." "Yes, it is," he heaves.

Mythril holds up a forefinger. "Give me a minute before we dissect," she expostulates.

"You're strong," Wolf goes on. "You know, your name means a metal that looks like silver but is stronger and lighter than steel."

"Never heard of it."

"Tolkien first wrote about it in Lord of the Rings. You haven't read the books?"

"No, I'm more into math and science. Although after my encounter with the note, I might reconsider some, some of my…hold on, my synapses seem to be misfiring."

Justin jogs to the kitchen to retrieve more cake and drinks. Being teenagers, they rebound faster than hounds on the trail of a shrewd double-back fox.

"Whew," says Mythril, "That's some note." Jerky breath. "What I'd wanted to do is run tests on it, maybe start out with simple x-rays. Wondered if it could be a hologram. But it's annoyingly complex, not something to be viewed lightly. Frankly, it'd probably flick off modern tests like so many gnats. So far," she reassures them, "it appears benign. Took me on an amazing trip, way back in our history and into the future." Hesitates. "I don't think an actual trip. Advanced telepathy? Scratch that. Not proven." Looks at Laura, "Whatever it is, this pains me to admit, but am pretty sure that one flashing glimpse was Cronos lit up like a rock star."

"Ha! Aha! Told ya," Laura.

"Yeah, yeah. Anyway, it didn't get around to telling me what it wants or why it's here, or why us. It does seem inordinately pleased with us, as a group or single unit, I mean. Urged me to get us into a circle."

"Hold it right there," says Justin. "We can't jump to its bidding without knowing more."

"No kidding," Laura. "We're dealing with time travel, no doubt about it, which has some appeal, but I don't want to be stuck in some caveman era no matter how cute the Flintstones. Certainly not in the middle of a Genghis Khan battle!!"

"It wants to have another meeting with me," says Myhril. "I haven't

29

committed to it."

"Do not," says Wolf firmly. "Not till we figure out a few things – the first test should be to ascertain if it can be trusted, but how?" he mutters. "Stuireadh." Then in a louder voice explains, "One who helps travelers get to where they need to be."

Justin suddenly turns. How could they forget? He puts the note back in the box. He's so flummoxed he waves at it shutting the lid. He could swear it smiled at him.

"The second test is to find out what the heck it wants," Wolf.

"This is extremely serious. Can we meet again tomorrow?" Ayes answer Justin.

"I'll walk Mythril home, make sure she's okay," Wolf holds out his hand to her. She's a bit wobbly on her feet.

Justin follows Laura out. She's frowning again. "When I was little, I had recurring dreams about magical faraway places," she tells him, kicking a pebble off the sidewalk. "I love fantasy books and fairy tales, so I thought it was because of them. Now I'm not sure. Do you suppose I could've been taken? On real trips? During the night? That's rather spooky.

"Oh, I also had a playground spring unicorn pony. We'd leap up into the atmosphere in the most breathless, exhilarating manner. She reached her stride in seconds. I attempted to call her Fleet Feet, but she didn't appear to like the name. I settled on Silver Lightning, Silly for short. She snorted, seemingly amused. I could hear her name for me in my mind, Spunky. Best friends, Silly and Spunky, attuned to the universe."

He squeezes her hand. "Given all that's going on, I'd say it's a real possibility." She shivers. "Between the four of us, we'll manage. We should start to think of it as an adventure." Gives her his lopsided grin and, to further distract her, changes the topic. "Remember how much fun we had playing Dungeons and Dragons?"

He's relieved when she smiles. "It was fun! Do you still have all your stuff? I kept mine. Hey, wanna play?"

30

****

Wolf and Mythril walk slowly, deep in thought. Finally, Mythril says, "How can we come up with a way to see if it's trustworthy?"

"We have to be careful. It signaled you out pretty dramatically. Scared me into the next universe!"

"It appeared to Laura first and, by extension, Justin. Laura and I didn't even know each other at the time. There has to be something about the four of us. We're all over the place with our diverse interests but do mesh well."

Wolf ponders. "Laura's a bit ditzy with her word fetish." Then, flustered by the connotation of the last word, he blurts out, 'I mean, not the other meaning of fetish but the definition with regard to magic. It's as if words for her are magical things to be admired or revered. They take on substance." Pausing as the idea takes shape. "Could they be capable of action?"

"Justin is a great photographer and not just technically. His photos are more than human interest. They capture an elusiveness beyond the immediacy of the subject. Beckon you to step into the images, to see further than the surface to what's…been left behind. It's hard to explain."

Mythril follows the thread of thought weaving through her consciousness. "Then there's you. You're an authority on ancient history and language."

Wolf shrugs.

"And then there's you, a math whiz." He says, looking at Mythril. "Remember, the note immediately attached itself to you and began to communicate. You were out of it for a while. Speaking of which, did it feel like a long time?"

"Nooo. I was too busy trying to sort fact from fiction. Felt as if I were trapped in a wonderful kaleidoscope, or prism. Animals, people, places, planets, stars, reflected with refracted light, spinning. The note pulled me out when I became too disoriented."

"Hmm," a crease between his brows, his eyes showing concern from behind his glasses.

"The main sensation was of wonder, awe. But also wonder as in wondering what the devil it's about. I did not have an impression of haste or anxiety, but there is definitely a thing we must do. I don't know what, but I do know it's important even if not imminently so. I could feel it. The note became agitated with Laura and Justin before they threw it unceremoniously into the box. It simply didn't want them to discard or forget it altogether. Remind me to tell them tomorrow. Guess we'll find out when I slap foreheads with the note again."

Wolf, grinning, "We shouldn't call it the note. It needs a dignified name."

"How about id est?"

"Great!!"

Standing on the sidewalk in front of Mythril's house, Wolf hesitates, then leans in to kiss her on her cheek. "See you tomorrow." "Sure thing," she breathes.

****

Justin steps onto Laura's porch preparatory to leaving for the night. "That was a load of fun," she beams. "Oh, this just occurred to me. We can't go on calling the note, the note. How about we name it Ergo?

"Ergo – hence, therefore?"

"Don't you think it fits?'

"Ergo it is, you i.e., you." Laughing, they embrace.

****

"Shall we take Ergo out of the box?" Justin asks.

"You mean id est?" Wolf. "We came up with id est."

"Good grief, this is pretty funny," Laura. "Let's cast votes. How about

32

putting them together? Ergo id est. Hence should come before that is, right?"

"I like it." "Good idea." "Has flair."

"We should vote on whether to let it, uh, Ergo id est, out. Hence that is, out. Out, damned spot," Laura finishes on a mutter.

"Don't insult Ergo till we know if she has a sense of humor," Mythril lectures.

"So now it's a she," Justin and Wolf simultaneously, smiling.

"Ergo, not it's. Of course, Ergo's a she though her new first name sounds masculine," concedes Laura.

"Oh, listen to yourself. Can you back that up with fact?" Justin quirks an eyebrow.

"I'm with Laura. Intuition, you know," Mythril. "So," with trepidation, "shall we let her out?"

They fall silent. Justin brings the box down from the closet shelf and places it on his desk. They stand around in stalemate for a few moments. The box begins to glow and emanate warmth, lulling the four into a mellow sense of safety. Justin blinks, looks at the other three in turn, and slowly reaches for the lid. As one, they draw in breath.

Instead of zooming out, the note crinkles its top margin into a smile, a smile with the cutest dimples. Mesmerized, they lean towards Ergo. The note elongates to make room for letters. "Greetings, earthlings. I am Ergo id est, so named by yourselves. Peace," a drawing similar to Spock's vee'd fingers appears. Laura takes charge, "Are you a missive from the planet Vulcan?" "I am an entity, not a missive. I know this planet of which you speak, but it is not my place of origin. The popular Star Trek television series and later the movies had some basis in fact, though their creator was not aware at the time. He may have had a thin, infinitesimal, nudge of glamour which enhanced his creativity. Not to cast aspersions on his imagination which was astounding."

33

Mythril, accusatory, "You frightened the H out of us the last time we opened the box."

"My humble apologies. I miscalculated your receptiveness and got ahead of myself, to put it in the vernacular. I did not mean to scare you."

"Okay," Mythril blows the stray hair out of her eyes. "May I ask why you're here?"

"A long story," Ergo continues to…type? scribble? the elegance of her script demands the term calligraphy. "I will reveal all incrementally so as not to startle you again. May I have a sip of liquid?"

"Of course…" Justin, quizzically. "Do you have honey?" "Honey?" he leaves. As Laura, Mythril and Wolf begin to bombard Ergo with questions, he returns. Ergo eagerly reaches, if that's the word, for the jar and absorbs it into her system. They can't tell how, but it's been sucked right out of the jar. They try to control their amazement, each adjusting their thought processes.

"Can we take a break to digest this information?" Wolf asks, aware that Mythril has paled.

"I'm sorry, of course," Ergo floats to her self-imposed sanctuary. The humans will soon realize she can exit the flimsy confinement whenever she wishes. As a matter of fact, over the last several months, she's done just that.

Mythril shakily takes a seat. The others plop onto chairs. Silence reigns, then they begin to jabber excitedly except for Mythril who leans her head back to stare at the ceiling.

Wolf notices, "Hey," and rubs her back in slow circles.

Mythril exhales, "I feel a little sick. I may upchuck." Scoots her chair back to place her head on her knees. "There go all my careful theories." A snort or maybe a sob escapes. "I don't know whether to laugh or cry."

Laura comes around to hug her. "C'mon. Where's that fierce spirit?"

"Blown to smithereens and floating in the sky like so much flotsam." Muffled.

"No, no, no. Don't throw out the theories with the bath water. All you do is ingurgitate, assimilate all this new data into what you know to be true. Or as true as can be known." She's tangled herself up.

Mythril starts to shake. Wolf murmurs sympathetically. Mythril looks up at him, howling laughter. "Oh, gawd," she tells Laura. Wipes her eyes, her ribs beginning to hurt. "Let's get down to business."

Relieved, they begin to hash things out, first what they've learned about Ergo id est. She has personality – whoa! Now, is this as true as can be known (everyone snorts), or has Ergo acquired her cute little traits (Laura's description) to charm them into thinking she's an ally or friend? An ally against what or whom? A friend for what reason? And what was all that about honey? Hold on, Justin remembers a jar or two of honey have vanished, which means…

"Ergo gets out of the box!"

"Not surprising. We've learned she's an interstellar traveler. Who knows what her capabilities are? Prior to that, we thought of her as a fancy confused message," Wolf observes.

"Right. The question begs itself, what's she been doing?" Laura.

"The question begs itself?" Justin throws her a sideways look.

She grins impishly. "If questions carry on conversations with themselves, the whole conversation must consist of questions. I wonder how a question would answer the original question? 'How are you this fine day?' 'I think I'm fine?' 'You think?' 'Do I think? Besides, didn't you use the word fine?'"

Justin gives her an affectionate noogie.

"This is normal," Mythril tells Wolf. "I never questioned my sanity before." Wolf grunts, "I don't know how you two get anything done with all the conversational tangents." "I began to enjoy the nonsense. It loosened up my thinking. Maybe I'll end up balancing science and whatever this turns out to be." He reaches for her hand, "Let me know if you need to be committed." "Promises, promises."

"Here's what we know-know," Laura picks up the gauntlet. "Ergo is a sentient being, not a missive. Rather, a sentient with a missive. She comes from a heck of a long way away. Parsecs?"

"Wow, Laura! Parsecs, yes," acknowledges Mythril.

"Her note form, form of note, ha, may not be what she actually looks like. Maybe she's huge, maybe microscopic. Perhaps she has a snout with tusks. No, a mouth like a bee, a honey bee." Laura is on a roll.

"Or she's what she seems, a note. She's incredibly impressive as a note, powerful, obviously able to get around, absorb honey," deadpans Justin. Laura smacks his shoulder.

"Right," interjects Wolf. "She may be willing to answer questions, if we can take her at face value. A paper at face value." He raises a laconic eyebrow at Mythril. "Let's draw up a list."

"Physical appearance," Mythril.

"Ability to shape shift," Laura.

"Her planet of origin, its galaxy or universe," Wolf.

"And its distance from earth," Justin.

"Her language and race history," Wolf, speculating.

"Reason for being here, the most important question," Mythril, insistent.

"Why honey?" Laura is frowning.

"I'd like to go on the journey with Mythril," says Wolf.

"Let's ask if we can all go together," Justin suggests. "Is everyone ready for this step?"

"Yes, but how do we prepare ourselves? What if we don't come back? What guaranty do we have?" asks Laura.

"We have to rely on blind faith," Mythril makes the bold statement, reversing roles with Laura.

"Yeah, there's no alternative. This is a being far more powerful than any human. She appears to be giving us a choice, but if she wants to take us, she will." Wolf points out.

"A polite paper sentient who guzzles honey," Laura is almost hysterical.

Taxed to exhaustion from the adrenaline rush, they break up the huddle, Justin automatically walks Laura home as Wolf and Mythril pair off in a most natural way.

At her porch, Laura says, "I wish Spock were real." "Maybe he is."

Chapter Six

It's a desultory group that meets in the school cafeteria the next day, all four with dark half-moons under a total of eight eyes, Laura counts. They pick at their food, stare glumly out the window. Mythril looks at Wolf who looks at Justin who looks at Laura who looks at Mythril, a silent round-robin. They agree they're too pooped to meet after school.

****

They all look better the next day at lunch. Justin starts off with, "I clarified something with Ergo," looking at Laura, "I asked, forcefully, that she reside elsewhere, not my closet and certainly not my room. She appears to be a note but who knows what she looks like or… Anyway, I became uncomfortable with her being there once we learned she can get about, and told her I need privacy and asked her to confine herself to the first floor. The last I saw she was in the laundry room sniffing detergent." "Oh, gee, I hadn't thought of that," Laura with consternation. "I know," Justin, grabbing her hand. "As soon as I reflected on it, I took immediate action." "Good," she says, "Really good." He goes on, "She did ask what privacy means. We had an extensive conversation about personal space – at first, she confused it with outer space which is apparently teeming with elbow to elbow populations on every habitable planet. But I pointed out the uniqueness of humans being social and private at once, hand-in-hand, so to speak."

Justin, back to the crux of the matter, "I have another question for Ergo. Is she working on her own or is she an ambassador? And my mind insists we test her, but how?"

"Don't think truth serum would work, unless she takes a corporeal form. There would still be the problem of dosage, her physiology and particular reactions, if she even consents! We cannot force her. Forget extrapolation. Nothing on earth could be contrasted or compared." Mythril looks at Laura, "This is a conundrum of the first order." Laura sniggers.

Wolf, tentatively, "We need another approach. A good faith request.

39

What if we ask her to demonstrate, say, something to benefit humankind? A medical advancement to cure deafness or severe depression or heart disease?"

Three pairs of eyes stare at him. "Excellent!" "Wonderful!" Mythril busses him on the cheek. Wolf flushes.

Justin, relieved, "Finally, we're getting somewhere. We should spend the week catching up on school projects and homework, so how about lunch at my house this Saturday? We need to figure out the logistics, how to approach the medical field. We can't barge in waving a calligraphy note." Laughter. Everyone's relieved as they get up to throw out trash and put away trays.

****

Laura, Mythril and Wolf tumble into Justin's house, buzzing excitedly, each carrying a honey jar. They're well-rested and relaxed with a concrete plan of action. Justin grins as he leads them into the kitchen. Elizabeth has a huge dish of paella, loaves of French bread, and fresh lemonade. The table's set, ready to go. They plop right down and begin to pass food around. Mmmm, mouths too full to speak, they give her thumbs up. She's a grand cook! It's 20 minutes before they pause. "Oh, gawd." "Thanks, I've never had better." "You should open a restaurant or cater!!" "I've thought of it," demurely. "Go for it!!" "We'd support you every day if we could afford it but will definitely order a couple times a week. My mom isn't the greatest cook (cough)." "Do not put it off, please!"

Elizabeth laughs, pleased with her son's friends, glad he has all of them but especially Laura.

The teenagers head for Justin's bedroom where they toss ideas back and forth as if they were multiple balls on a tennis court.

"What I think," Justin says, "is that we should broach the medical benefit thing to Ergo first, explain we need a good faith reason to work with her, tell her we need to come up with a pitch that does not involve extraterrestrials because we'd come across as short in the attic."

40

"Great, well thought out," says Wolf. The girls nod.

****

Ergo beams up at him. "I knew you four were the correct choice. Intelligent, curious, intrepid."

They bow in unison, smiling ear to ear, all eight ears, Laura notes. She has to keep on top of her game.

"I intuit you have questions, tests. Please proceed," Ergo's expression amused.

"Alright," Wolf. "We have several questions but first, we'd like to ask you to show good faith. Can you provide humanity with a boon, say, a cure for deafness or depression?"

Laura, regaining some of her natural levity, "On a small scale to start, not global. There'd be riots if everyone ill with depression were to suddenly go around like smiling emoticons." Justin's lips thin to keep from laughing, but his dimples give him away.

Ergo crinkles a nod, rapidly calligraphing. "Of course, how do you wish to proceed?"

Laura, sidetracked, "Is your true state that of a calligraphist, or can you manifest yourself in other forms? Wait, did you take on the shape of a 'noted' calligraphist the better to catch my attention since I heart words?" Justin's eyes twinkle at her choice of language.

"Yes, I did," Ergo ascertains easily while she tries to absorb the use of the word heart in this context as Laura rolls her eyes at the revelation.

Mythril latches onto the important noun, "Emissaries. Why? Where? How?" Straight for the jugular, Wolf notes with pride.

Ergo flattens, then straightens. "I am able to take on different physical forms as suits the mission. You are not ready to see me in my original body. Your human eyes would melt, resemble colors in a crayon vat." The newly appointed ambassadors eye one another. The air crackles with apprehension. Crayons in a Crayola vat? Ewww. The yuck factor

41

outweighs the scary. "You will acquire the ability to look upon me much later. Meanwhile, I will heart words with you." Her awkward use of the word lightens their mood so much, they begin to chortle, then laugh with only a tinge of hysteria.

Ergo blushes, the pink creeping up her parchment. It's Laura who tries to hug her before she realizes she'd wrinkle her and pats a corner instead. "We heart you," she tells Ergo. "Is that another definition?" "Yes, it means we like you. I vote you can be trusted." "But," inserts Mythril, slits for eyes, "you still must pass our test."

"Okie-dokie. Is this word usage correct?"

Laura is beside herself, "Patois! You're doing extremely well. Slang is a beast." Carefully high-fives a corner with a pinkie. Ergo mimics the motion but, oops, ends up giving Laura a stinging paper cut. Justin kisses the ya-ya.

"Gawd, you don't mean slang is an animal, right?"

"It is if it bites you in the patootie. Patootie-fruity. And did you just say gawd, not god? Wow! Bow to a cow!"

Myrhtil smacks her forehead, gives Ergo a sympathetic look which Ergo totally appreciates. Wolf raises his eyebrows, melodramatically looks at the ceiling. Justin hugs Laura.

Mythril briskly commands, "Can we puhleeze get back to business."

Wolf camouflages his need to touch her with a simple high-five. He turns to Ergo, "We need to discuss the logistics of providing medical relief to people with clinical depression. First, explanation of your treatment to the medics. Second, how we coach it so they believe it is a viable approach without raising suspicion."

"Easy-peasy," Ergo flaunts her expanding vernacular fecundity, the words sprouting like weeds. Groan follows groan around the table. "The treatment consists of emanations from me. Lookie-see, our technology is far more advanced than that of earth. Millennia past we discovered DNA manipulations to bypass depression, addiction, aberrant behavior, deformities, disease, you name it. One eventual side effect of this was peace. Peace. Inconceivable!" Pauses. "Our mission is to spread the benefits of our technology. Incidentally, we prefer recruiting help from the inhabitants of each planet, where feasible, so as not to abuse our powers or exploit any vulnerability."

Mythril with a piercing gaze, "Emanations. Radiological, laser?"

"Something we call mythrical." Points to Mythril. "As a pure scientist, you recoil at the mention of what you humans call magic. However," strongly, "so-called magic is rooted in science. In your history, magic was erroneously linked with witches, druids, the occult, whatever was handy, to a largely ignorant populace desperate to explain natural phenomena."

Mythril and Laura exchange glances.

"As for bringing the medical community to heel, all I do is mesmerize them."

Laura casts Mythril a complacent look. "Ah, as in mesmerism."

"Yeah. Yeah," Ergo savors the word.

Wolf states, "And the results are permanent. No reversal to original problems."

"Absofrigginlutely," Ergo's on a roller coaster.

"Okay," Justin cracks his knuckles. "This city is big enough to have several psychiatric clinics. Can you call around first thing Monday to evaluate their professionalism?"

"Cool beans," Ergo, gleefully.

"Just how powerful are you? Can you mesmerize them over the phone?"

"Pshaw." She doesn't give Wolf an immediate answer; rather, she is briefly silent. "Done. I have a meeting Monday morning, 8:00 a.m."

Stunned, they gasp in unison. She says matter-of-factly, "The Titans were babies in diapers."

43

Mythril grabs onto one word, "Were. They did exist but are no longer? Or did they evolve into something else when they outgrew their diapers?"

"In the grand scheme of things, Titans were in the nursery room of evolution. They're no longer here; they're elsewhere," cryptically.

Laura pipes up, "Good night, fright. Are humans a subspecies?"

"Not exactly. Humans are struggling to get out of the mud pond, so to speak. Bleak."

Mythril accuses Laura, "I hope you've only corrupted her speech, not her brain."

Justin holds up a hand, "My brain is ready to explode. Let's take a break." Ergo declines to join them, as she puts it, "for the nonce." He doesn't bother putting her in the box. "Please keep your presence on the qt." "qt?" "Hush-hush." "Hush-hush?" "Secret, clandestine." "Gotcha," she agrees cheerfully. "Gotcha?" he teases. They jog to the kitchen for ice cream sandwiches. Two or three each refuels their energy enough to leave.

Chapter Seven

Justin and Laura grab hands to head to her house as Mythril and Wolf stroll off, hands in pockets. It takes less than a block for Mythril to quietly turn, admire Wolf's profile, the strong jaw, straight nose, sculpted lips. A shock of blond hair covers half his forehead. She can't see those piercing blue-green eyes. She knows them to be there, right behind his glasses. His hands remain firmly crammed in the pockets of his jeans, but something lurks in his face. She clears her throat, stumbles around in her mind, pops her bubble gum. He absently pops his which he never does for obvious reasons.

"That was some session," she squeaks. "Hmm," he responds, clearing his own throat, his mind clearly elsewhere. She pushes on, "Mesmerism, Titans in diapers, pond humans." He visibly reels his mind to the conversation, "Er, crayola vats." They smile as they walk up to her porch. "Well," she says lamely as they face off. They blunder or pitch forward. He leans to kiss her cheek. She grabs the back of his neck. Subtlety will only get you so far. Their mouths painfully crash together. When they gasp, her bubble gum sticks to his braces. Mfft. They reluctantly pull apart, the gum a sticky bridge looping them together. Two steps backwards, the gum hangs in there. Of all the…they burst out laughing, cross their eyes to look at the sweet connection. They advance. The long loop falls to their clothing like an obsessed bungee jump. She reaches out to scrape off his braces. His thumb wipes the gum off her teeth and lips. Ugh. By the time they overcome the ridiculous debacle, they're doubled over.

"The bubble gum part was gross, sorry" gasps Wolf, "But the kissing. Amazing doesn't begin to describe it." "A gross romantic story," she agrees, reaching for him with the observation it was the best ice breaker ever in the history of the poor human race. Of course, bubble gum per se wasn't always around. Tree sap, that was it, also used as toothpaste. The curious part of her brain that won't quit wonders if prehistoric man had had the same experience. The majority of her brain never left Wolf.

As he reluctantly departs, he suggests The Four and Ergo meet at his house that weekend.

****

Ergo's results amaze the psychiatric community, excitement rippling through the medical community faster than shooting stars.

****

Mythril cautions her friends in a low voice, "We're too excited, intense. A few classmates are beginning to wonder what we're up to."

Laura casually looks around. "We're teenagers. Teenagers are excitable, high energy."

Wolf points out, "We're nerds. We're supposed to be intense."

"But you're also correct, Mythril. I've heard some whispers, nothing specific, but consider furrowed brows with looks cast in our direction. We need to tone it down a wee bit, nothing drastic," says Justin.

"You're not suggesting we infiltrate the "in" crowd?!" Laura gasps.

Justin throws his head back, "That would be drastic. No, how about going to the upcoming school dance." Holds his breath.

Laura, "Is this the first time you've had this idea?" Justin smiles knowingly. Wolf slams his head into the table before he realizes he'd be dancing with Mythril. Mythril eyes him as the same thought engulfs her.

They think it over as they eat lunch. "It means we'd have to buy dresses," Laura gapes at Mythril, "And shoes to go with. I'm not doing my nails, or my hair. And absolutely no make-up!" Myrthril nervously grabs her napkin, shreds it into itty-bitty pieces, completely freaked out, speechless for the second time in her life. Laura addresses the guys, "You aren't immune. You'll need fancy clothes, too, just so you know," she adds, lining up her you's. She's throwing letters into her next painting. "I don't think tuxes are called fancy clothes," Justin, and to Wolf, "We'd need to buy corsages." Wolf is taken aback. He's not the only one. They're all in shock. This is harder than math, Laura admits as she mulls over the formality of dress. She brightens when she looks at Justin till she notices he

46

looks like he's about to have a heart attack. "If you don't want to…" she starts, but he tells her it's fine. Much more than fine, he reassures her while his brain stutters, *Wonder what she'll look like in a gown?* Mythril is quick on the uptake, *More complicated than bubble gum, but look at that outcome*, merrily. Wolf, *More complicated than bubble gum, but look at that outcome*, at once cheerful.

No need to say anything. Yes takes it.

****

"You want to what?!" exclaims the cheerleader who handles the dance tickets. "We want four tickets to the dance," asserts Justin. She stares at the handsome duo, shaken. Then regretfully, "You're not taking Laura and Mythril, are you?" "They would be The Chosen Ones," Wolf leans over to affirm soto voce the double meaning, not that she'd have an inkling. Justin notes, "We're extremely lucky dudes," the word strange on his tongue.

"Dudes?" Wolf as they walk down the hall.

"Threw a curve ball at her cause she was rude, but it didn't come off quite like I wanted. On top of the futility of it, the blasted word singed my tongue."

Wolf claps him on the shoulder. "I usually don't understand common syntax, shall we say, either. You know how some people use sentences made up almost entirely of man, like, dude. Not to be judgmental since they seem to communicate well enough. I simply don't get it."

****

Laura slumps after the third dress she tries on. She shops twice a year for jeans, shorts, undies and shoes because of growth spurts, not because she bloody enjoys it. Her mom always caves in to her request to take measurements and sallies forth to buy tops and jackets, sneaking in a skirt or sundress which makes Laura feel guilty enough to wear on occasion.

Mythril has tried on precisely three dresses, as well, almost ripping the last one as she flings it off. "We better get out of here before we're arrested for clothes abuse." "Mall department stores suck," agrees Laura. A dim light bulb flickers somewhere behind her brain. "Ohh, there's a boutique store on Main Street, not far from the ice cream shop," she wiggles her brows. They escape without making eye contact with the salesclerk; mumbled thanks should suffice. Fortified by banana splits, they walk a couple blocks when Laura exclaims dramatically, "Alors." They've reached the chic blue door to Voila!

A bell tinkles melodiously as they enter; a delicate incense wafts through the air. The girl behind the counter smiles in relaxed greeting. Goth, steampunk, and vintage items are casually displayed to advantage. Mythril lets out a reluctant sigh, *Never before have I bothered with apparel but this, this calls to me.* She fingers a velvet indigo mid-calf dress with a silvery lace overskirt. Modest cap sleeves are countered by a lacy bodice insert that hints at cleavage. The kicker for her is the chain mail cincher. She snatches it off the hanger. Laura has a frothy multicolored salmon, orange and pink striped concoction over a pale green sheath. Sleeveless, strapless, low-backed. She's hit the sherbet jackpot.

For the first time they're anxious to use a mirror. And, wow, if they do say so themselves.

"What shoes would go with these dresses?" Mythril to the clerk. "Ankle boots." She retrieves them, one pair black lace-up, the other pale green suede with Velcro closures. Both low-heeled. "Thank the goddess," says Laura. "I've never worn heels." Mythril gives her a high five. They purchase black ruffle-topped socks and off they go after sending text messages to their male accomplices.

Justin and Wolf disgustedly leave the mall. Really?! Ding, ping, incoming messages. "We need to discuss style," Laura's, and Mythril's, "You guys free?" Alright.

They're always free for the "gels." (Wolf couldn't pronounce girl when he was a kid.)

"Here's what we got since formal gowns made us sick to our stomachs. I don't know if there's a store with this style for guys. Maybe Amazon?" Laura, anxiously. "I'm not wearing a top hat. Otherwise, cool." declares

Justin. "A minimal look for me, too," Wolf, "Leather vest with a few studs in nod to Mythril's chain mail - white shirt, linen trousers, a flowing blue cravat. Okay?" Mythril throws her arms around him.

"Do we know how to dance?" Justin, suddenly struck. "Only ballet which does teach the one-two pause-on-three waltz step," Laura says. "Oh, crap," says Mythril. Wolf shakes his head vehemently. Their parents could probably teach them the boogie, their grandparents the fox trot, the Charleston.

"We could sit out the hip hop and other stuff. Plenty to talk about what with Ergo. I'll teach you the waltz. Can't be hard to shuffle in place to the other slow dances," Laura.

Justin drives his mother's old clunker to pick up Laura. He stops breathing when she descends the stairs. Her hair is piled up with irresponsible tendrils cascading around her face. No make-up necessary, she has but pale pink lip gloss. She's a vision of curvy loveliness in that crazy dress, her dainty ankles supported by bootees. She concentrates on walking. The heels are low, but she has zilch experience outside of sandals and sneakers. She looks up when she reaches the bottom step.

Eeek! All Laura's cells scramble deliciously. *Cobblestones and crystals, I know he's handsome, but this takes the cake. Bakes the cake. Icing. Get a grip. Blink your lids, kids.* Her lids obey but hold the blink before popping open.

Talk about mesmerism, total. They come together in a rush of molecules. They're peripherally aware her parents have entered the room. Justin clears his throat, remembers the corsage. He fumbles with the pale pink rose on a green ribbon. He's yet to achieve speech. Instead he indicates with a circling motion that she turn. He carefully places the rose in the hollow of her throat and ties the ribbon in back, then puts his hands on her waist to twirl her back to face him. They smile goofily. Laura's parents advance, her mother to kiss her and her dad to shake Justin's hand. As they leave, her parents are hugging. No words have been exchanged.

On the porch they kiss breathlessly before they head out to pick up

Mythril and Wolf at Mythril's house.

Wolf's almost literally knocked over by Mythril when she enters the room. Unlike Justin, he can find his vocal cords but actual words elude him. "D-duh, w-wha, y-you". She saves him by striding across the room and grabbing him by the back of the neck to kiss him before her parents emerge from the back of the house. That kiss jolts his weakened brain. Cohesive speech gathers itself on the distant horizon.

By the time sequined Ergo joins the four at the entrance to the gym, they can and do speak in jerky sentences

Ergo tucks herself into Wolf's vest pocket to observe goings-on as a folded pseudo handkerchief. The beat of the music has her moving. "Zowers, this is the bomb," she communicates telepathically. Nervous tension disappears as the group laughs. They find seats and the guys head off in search of refreshments.

Their relaxed exuberance and unusual clothes garner attention. A girl next to Mythril turns to look her up and down. "Where did you get your outfit? Almost looks like a costume but so original for a school dance. I like it." "Oh," Mythril replies airily, "There's this little boutique, Voila! on Main." Remembers Ergo, "It's the bomb." The girl leans forward to check out Laura's dress. "Love your dress, too, and I saw those bootees when you walked over. They are the cutest things." Laura takes a second to respond, not used to this type of conversation. "Thanksgiving." The girl looks startled. "I mean, thanks." Tries to save the conversation, "Is there a donation giving, a gift to be given? You know, a charity at the door?" Mythril coughs to cover her laugh. The girl, "Not that I know of, but that's a really good idea. I'm a member of an organization that helps the less fortunate. Food, clothing, scholarships. It's not school affiliated, but I bet the principal would be interested. By the way, I'm Sarah. Do you mind if my date and I remain at this table?" Leans over, "He's a bit reclusive. You're both so open, I think he'd feel more comfortable around you." They nod assent just as Justin and Wolf return. Introductions reveal her date's name is John. Sarah and John, nice innocuous names until it's learned John is an Air Force cadet and Sarah plans to enroll next year with the goal of becoming a fighter pilot. At this, Ergo rustles in Wolf's pocket. She'd prick her ears if she had them. She files their names in her memory bank for future, ahem, use.

Conversation becomes animated as the six get to know one other. It's nice to make friends with two intelligent, easy-going schoolmates with a different set of skills.

Ergo alternates between soaking in the party atmosphere, trying not to jiggle Wolf's pocket when the music moves her, and inserting telepathic messages here and there. "There are no 'one-eyed, one-horned, flying purple people eaters,'" she asserts. The next song prompts, "I suppose 'I'd go the whole wide world, I'd go the whole wide world, I'd go the whole wide world just to find her,' is ironic or tongue in cheek, the poor singer searching for the eternally illusive only girl for him that his mom told him was out there." She concludes to herself, *I have to say humans are an interesting species*.

Sarah and John are not privy to her mental tidbits although they begin to notice the other four periodically halt mid-sentence, as if deep in thought. Sarah whispers to John, "They are the top brains in this school." "Ahh," enlightened, "You're no slouch yourself." "Nor you, but we're both more mechanical minded," she answers.

The DJ puts on a slow dance. John reaches for Sarah's hand and they stand up.

Justin and Wolf eye their respective dates. They head for the middle of the dance floor, the better to hide, but all those practice sessions make for relaxed dancing. Even Ergo drifts in her sanctuary as she thinks drowsily, *This is as good as taking an existential break.*

Chapter Eight

Ergo wonders about their physical reaction to her standard poof! mode of transport and decides to limit it to one short trip. "The first thing we must do is obtain a flying vehicle," irrevocably. She explains calligraphy was her choice of first communication but is switching to mental telepathy. "We can't waltz into a hangar and take one," Justin answers dreamily, the pleasant memory of the waltz at his cerebral forefront. "Of course not, but there are plane junk yards," comes Ergo's placid response. "We can't trespass, either, or involve ourselves in grand theft!" Wolf exclaims. Ergo, intoxicated with slang, asserts, "Aww, cool your jets. And, yes, we can when it comes to the welfare of all humans." Her argument is persuasive as medics are busy with documentation of the incredible reversals of depression. It's somehow become general knowledge that treatments are due to DNA manipulation. Foggy since no one's stepped forward with an eye to the Nobel Prize, but there can be no denial of the results. They have yet to realize this new treatment will effectively put them out of business.

They agree to her plan, unable to refute her argument.

Teleportation is alarmingly effective though quite uncomfortable with nausea and vertigo as they hit the ground in an unceremonious heap. Recuperation takes roughly an hour. Ergo is alarmed.

Finally, they note they have arrived in a large field. They gaze about to see a vast number of planes. A plain of planes, thinks Laura. They trudge through endless rows of rusting machinery. Justin silently clasps her hand. She feels empathy for the discarded inanimate objects.

The hot and dusty afternoon nears sunset when they come across a small airplane. It's sleek in design, supersonic as they imagine supersonic to be. As they circle it, the craft begins to shimmer. Rust falls away, engines hum. Holy She! They step back as a warm sensation washes over them. Ergo radiates approval.

They undulate into the craft as if on a wave. Ergo turns to Laura and asks her to close her eyes and concentrate on the words to get them home.

Laura gawks at her. "You can do this," Ergo confirms, "You have such a reverence for words that from your mouth they can morph into action. Deep in your subconscious, you recognize this truth." Laura frowns in consternation. "Give yourself time to acknowledge your power."

Dimly through a floating sensation, Laura hears Ergo exhort Justin to open a portal. "Use your photography skills. Imagine a strip of negatives and how to open one. Mentally reach for Laura, coordinate your portal with her transport destination." Justin frowns in concentration. Laura reaches for him with her mind. Nebulous at first, words begin to link with the sketchy opening he projects.

Ergo instructs Mythril, "Use your mythril namesake to lightly chain everyone together." Mythril shuts her eyes, makes an effort to slow down her erratic breathing, reaches deep into her soul, if soul it is, till she feels a warmth begin to pulsate. She jerks away, then chastises herself and tries again. She somehow feels Wolf, Laura and Justin on a plane not physical. She wraps herself around them.

Ergo waits a moment then applauds, "Excellent!" In an aside to Wolf, "Your talents will come into play later. Sit back and enjoy the ride."

Laura sinks deep into her psyche, her hand tightly held by Justin. She begins to form words, letter by letter. H, then o followed by m. She comes to an abrupt stop. *Oh, my great goddess!* They can't land in her house! She hastens to erase the letters – who cares how it works - and starts again. M y parents' yar. *Oops, Better make that backyard.* Quickly, my parents' backyard. Poof. They peer out the windows. Faint moonlight bathes the weeping willow, a gentle breeze cradling the branches in a sweet lullaby. There's the sycamore with the tire swing. *Whew.*

They shakily unfasten safety belts. Gathering their scattered thoughts, Justin voices a concern, "We need to camouflage the ship." "Yes, Navigator and Second-in-Command," Ergo answers theatrically, embracing the human trait. Her grin, like the sliver of a blazing horizontal sun, splits her "face" ear to ear. "If all of you will step outside to see our galactic ship!"

When they emerge to look back at the area they see no more than a faint emanation of silvery light. Laura does a golf clap, "Epic! I name this ship Oisin." Wolf answers Justin's raised eyebrow, "Oisin is a handsome poet of ancient Ireland. In one legend he travels with the fairy Niamh to the Otherworld land of promise, or land of the young." Mythril begins to roll her eyes but remembers Laura transported them back using words! She frowns. *How could words...?!* Wolf notes her distress and drapes an arm over her shoulders.

Justin arranges a meeting at his house the coming weekend.

****

Stunned at the awesomeness of their feat, they attempt to embrace the normalcy of classes and homework, maintaining this façade the whole week. But beneath the surface is the seething anxiety and excitement of stupendous things about to happen.

Almost timidly, Laura, Mythril and Wolf enter Justin's house. *Backbone*, Laura chides herself. *Don't tiptoe.*

A hasty lunch of sandwiches and lemon water. Justin opens the laundry room to beckon Ergo.

She addresses them, "This journey will take us back in time, a short trip as time travel goes. You need to be at ease so decide when and where."

Silence, then Laura, hesitantly, "I'd like to travel to the time of the gods, but that would be quite a leap. So first maybe Ireland during Brian Boru's lifetime. I believe he was the last High King of Ireland. It is thought by some that he ended Viking occupation but Vikings never conquered Ireland. Instead, many of them assimilated into the Irish culture, embracing Christianity and intermarrying. I've always been intrigued by him, probably since I first heard the instrumental, *Brian Boru's March*. He died an old man in 1014, but I'd like to arrive in 940 or thereabouts to see him as a child or young man."

Mythril nods her head, "Yes. The country is such an interesting mythical cauldron of elves, faeries, leprechauns, selkies, banshees." Laura raises a brow. Mythril plows on, "We can check out this Boru paragon along with

55

all the alleged magic, then jump from Brian Boru's time to the ancient Druids of Great Britain and Gaul. They were philosophers, teachers, judges, supposedly mediators between humans and the gods. Magic, too. I'd love to do a spot of research while in the area if there's time." This last tongue-in-cheek. Laura stares, impressed.

"And go back further to see who put up those giant Stonehenge boulders," suggests Wolf.

"That'd be a worthwhile investigation!" Normally unflappable Justin says excitedly. He spins to Ergo, "I can take my photography equipment? Would love to do a documentary on how Stonehenge was raised. Hmm, no one would believe I was actually there." Thinks for a moment, "I could tweak the images so they appear to come from my imagination."

"We'll be arriving in a modern flying device, so, yes, you may take your equipment," Ergo, drily.

Justin suggests several things to address. "How long in real time, our time, will this journey take? We have school and extracurricular activities and, most importantly, we can't freak our parents out by disappearing for any great length of time. Which leads to a big question, we will return with no mental or physical changes?"

"Yeah," says Mythril, "while I have an interest in druids, I refuse to become one."

Wolf tweaks her cheek.

"Or a blood-thirsty Irish king," mutters Laura, twirling Justin's nape hair with a finger. "Glad you don't want to become male," he cheekily replies.

"Ears here," Ergo admonishes as Wolf wiggles his ears. *Humans, interesting but so immature.*

Laura pipes up, "Will we be disguised as trees, banshees, leprechauns? How is this going to work?"

"You will wear cloaks that render you invisible. That's the upside. The downside is you have to step lively to avoid bumping into people because they will feel you. Do not insert yourselves into a battle, fisticuffs, soldier exercise; you will be hurt!! While I can resuscitate you, 'twould be painful. A plus is you may speak freely to one another as they will not hear you, but no singing or whistling in Ireland. They are such a lively bunch and will pick automatically up on music."

"Wait, just wait. This has to be how myths and legends started!" Mythril says triumphantly.

"Not exactly." Ergo is mysterious. Laura and Mythril exchange glances.

Justin reins Ergo in, "So the time frame? And we'll be the same on return? Ourselves?"

"We'll spend a week in each location which translates to an afternoon in this time. Absolutely you will come back as funnily human as when you left."

"Funnily. Not funnel-y, shaped like a funnel after going through a, what, time funnel? Oh, forget that, we'll go through Justin's film portal," Laura sarcastically.

Ergo sighs gustily enough to stir the air. *Earth gods, give me strength.*

Justin has another question, "How will going back in time help with our work as emissaries?"

Ergo is glad after all she chose these four. "When you zoom around the galaxies helping species beat disease, you will be faced with all kinds of mythological belief systems. It will be easier if you can move freely within the historical context of each planet before you attempt to manipulate DNA. View this trip to your own history as job initiation."

Laura gulps, "When do we embark?"

"How about a week from today."

Laura, serious, nods at Justin. Mythril, "Okay." Wolf, "May as well bite the bullet."

Ergo, "It's not all work. It'll be fun, too."

Chapter Nine

The air is staccato and electric with opposing feelings of trepidation and elation. As soon as they are seated, the engines thrum. They buckle up, adjust helmets and communication devices. Ergo explains they need to become familiar with the gadgets and tools asap (her tongue lingers to savor the acronym) as they will need to be prepared for any contingency when they fly without her once fully trained. Laura and Justin hold hands as they coordinate time and place. Oisin responds to commands with a baritone brogue. Wolf looks up from his tome on language. "So you're Irish," he addresses the ship. "Aye," responds Oisin, "and what is it you are reading there?' Wolf holds up the book. Oisin grunts, "I thank ye for yer interest in me country." Laura and Justin grin. Mythril is absorbed jotting equations.

It's tree instead of three when Oisin counts down. How cute, Laura thinks. The launch is effortless. In a twinkling they are floating at tremendous speed through corridors of fractured crystal, lights, prisms, hazy reflections interspersed with images of people in different garb, animals, foliage, buildings, villages, pristine valleys, streams, mountains, rotating seasons, distant stars, galaxies. But something becomes terribly wrong as they find themselves in a screaming, whirling, slamming vortex when Laura's mind suddenly careens about. She appears to have lost focus! Well, it *is* her first attempt.

The craft jerks to a stop. Oisin lifts his hatch. The occupants slowly emerge into an ominous mist. Unexpectedly, the air is pierced by a primordial scream and as the atmosphere clears on the horizon there appears the shape of a velociraptor. "I hope this is the set of Jurassic Park and not the real thing," Justin whispers. Urgently, "To the ship!" Slowly they edge backwards. As Oisin slams the hatch, the raptor strikes the hull with tremendous force. "Justin," screams Laura, "A portal, quick!" In his anxiety, Justin comes up with a positive film portal instead of a negative. "Crap!," curses Laura. "Watch your language," Ergo admonishes her. "'Watch your language?!' That's all you have to say?!" snaps Wolf. Laura and Justin are too busy with coordinates to pay attention. Once they're underway, however, the humans turn to scowl at Ergo. "You handled my test well," she beams. "You mean to say you deliberately sidetracked us?! Don't ever piss us off like that again!" growls Justin, pointing an accusing finger at her. She smiles serenely which just makes his scowl more fierce.

Shortly Oisin calls out, "Wakey, wakey. We have arrived. Since this is our destination, we will go no furder. Please take care as you exit the craft." Wolf pats the console.

"Wait!!" Mythril uncharacteristically screams. Taken aback, even calm Oisin lurches.

"Merde," spits Ergo in a Picardish way as Wolf grabs Mythril, brows furrowed. "Don't bedevil me," she scolds Mythril.

"Perfidy and pink pants!! What bit you?" yells Laura.

"We forgot to pick up Einstein! We have to go back." Mythril is almost hyperventilating. Laura sighs, nods to Ergo. "She's right."

Humans could be a pain in the glutes. Ergo commands everyone to prepare for flight and, bypassing Justin and Laura to speed things up, gives Oisin the okay for a basic time space u-turn. *Ha*, petulantly. *Yikes, I'm taking on human traits.*

The scientist is - where else? - in his lab, formulas scribbled on the blackboard behind him. Sockless, disheveled, dressed in his signature suit with a vest over an adorable little paunch, his white hair gently waving about, eyes closed, he's playing Mozart on his violin. Mythril walks over. When he reaches the natural end of the composition and opens his eyes, she takes a jerky breath. "You once said if not for physics, you'd be a musician." He nods. "I see my life in terms of music. I live my daydreams in music." "Annus mirabilis," she murmurs, "1905, the miracle year." "There are many things we can discuss," he concurs.

Ergo makes an appearance before them. "I dislike interrupting the gabfest, but we must be going."

Einstein is puzzled. Mythril turns to him. "We are from the near future. Ergo here is an advanced species from another planet." Einstein looks at Ergo's form. "Weird, huh?" Mythril giggles as Ergo huffs. "You were right

60

about space and time, of course. We're on our way to Ireland in the time of Brian Borus. I'll explain on our way, if you're willing? Of course, you're willing!" And with that, Mythril loops her arm through his as he smiles in delight.

****

"Before we leave Oisin, I will shift into a more comfortable form." They gape as Ergo flickers. There's a small pop before a creature resembling a housecat, roughly twice as large, stands archly before them. Elliptical vertical irises take center stage in beautiful amber eyes. Her tail slinks back and forth in slow hypnosis. Her coat is a ripple of forest green. Laura is first to find her voice. "Why did you make yourself known as a curlicued note? What is the meaning of *Tuesday Was Two Days Ago?*" Peering closely at Ergo's amazing eyes, "Ah, the note is elliptical, oblique, as well?"

"Proud I am of this small intrigue." She's obviously seen Star Wars. "I confess the ruse was an admirable way to get your attention." Her smile is feline.

Imperturbable Einstein puts his pipe in his mouth.

"You said we aren't ready to see you in your original form. This," continues Laura, gesturing to the body before her, "is temporary?"

"Oh, yes, you will not see my natural state for another couple of centuries." Eight eyebrows disappear into four hairlines. Einstein puffs away.

Justin, making an effort at diversion from this last statement, "What the hell was the honey about?" Three pairs of eyes swing towards him at the crude word.

"Oh, that. Simple, really. My cultural research of a planet usually begins with literature for the wee ones," glances towards the console. "The first book I happened upon was *Winnie the Pooh*. Pooh Bear is a lovable, if not smart, lumbering furry animal whose main goal in life is to eat honey. When I experimented with the gooey delicacy, I became addicted for a time. Thank the galaxies I was able to kick the habit with sunflower seeds."

Mythril, "How in the planet…" smacks her forehead "did you eat seeds?!"

Ergo smiles conspiratorially, "Shapeshifting." Goosebumps leap onto Laura's skin.

"Now," briskly, "any other questions before we take leave of Oisin? No? A few pointers before we go, then.

"Remember you are invisible but not invincible. By the way, you will be masked by mist-like invisibility cloaks here on earth when time traveling but not other planets. You won't be the oddest things out there." Several eyes roll. "I will be invisible to the people of this time, but not to you. No matter how interesting you find this journey, be vigilant. Periodically check to make sure you know where I am." She is solemn. "Am I clear?"

"Clear as glass," says Laura.

Hmm, another phrase to memorize. "Okay, Oisin," nodding to the console.

Chapter Ten

The hatch lifts soundlessly. Ergo suddenly appears outside the craft. Justin takes the first wave out, pivots to assist Laura. Wolf exits, Mythril's hand on his shoulder. They turn to assist Einstein. Looking about, they find themselves in a valley surrounded by breathtaking emerald hills dotted with small clouds. No, not clouds. Sheep. A cool breeze ruffles past with an occasional hint of…manure. Scudding sheep, uh, clouds alleviate the blue of the sky. Small dwellings can be seen in the distance.

Ergo gives them a few moments to view their surroundings before crooking her tail in invitation to follow. They set out on the rocky trail bordered by a clear stream. There must be trout in the indigo depth of its pools. The landscape is the stunning 50 shades of green Justin had heard about. Stone and hedge walls mark livestock boundaries backed by dense forest. The heartbeat of the trees is more felt than heard.

Buoyed by a sense of freedom, lightness settles on the group. Laura glances back at Mythril who sports an expression of awe. "You feel it," whispers Laura. Mythril grins, "I don't know what it is, but, yes." The hike is so wonderful, they barely notice the village before them until they hear unearthly squeals. Ergo calls a halt. "What the blazes is that?!" demands Wolf, wishing he had a sword. *My poor innocent lambs.* Ergo launches into an explanation. "We've arrived on Market Day. That was the sound of a pig being slaughtered." "Gross." "Eww." "My god." Wolf utters, "Jesus, Maria y Jose."

"Delicious when roasted," observes Ergo.

Justin is cynical, "You eat meat?"

"In this form, I do."

Justin mutters, "Honey, sunflower seeds, meat."

"The language spoken is Gaelic. Will you understand it?" Ergo addresses Wolf. He nods enthusiastically. "Very well, I will enable the translation device for the rest of you."

Despite the awesomeness of time travel, Mythril can't help starting a conversation with Einstein, beginning with his classic 1905 annus mirabilis articles which apparently planted physics on its backside.

Laura listens with half an ear as they drone on about inertia of a body (whose body?), energy content (energy is happy?), light emission and transformation, cathode rays, atoms, electrons, electromagnetic something or other, molecular kinetic theory. She's about to sleep on her feet before a collaboration with Justin incorporating photography with art using random words and letters begins to form in the thing she fondly calls her brain.

Engrossed with his conversation with Mythril, Einstein bumps into a country gentleman.

The man turns to address his companion, "Eis McSquard, watch where you're going, man." The man thus addressed, glares, "Give me some space or your time will be considerably shortened."

Einstein draws in a breath. Ergo rears to place a paw on his leg in warning.

Eis McSquard? What?! He ponders as the group advances toward the tables burdened with food, trinkets, utensils, herbs. Ergo shapeshifts to a woman in a dress of modest means, a basket on her hip. She purchases meat, bread, honey, meathe, and surreptitiously beckons the group to the side of a building at a short distance. Justin questions the drink. Ergo assures him of its low alcoholic content. *Ohhkay.*

An hour later, he's pleasantly relaxed. Laura smiles liquidly at him. Aw, hell, their first time journey and he's already made a huge mistake, hic.

Ergo approaches, felinely graceful in movement. "It is rumored by *The Village Vine*, i.e., word of mouth, Brian Boru will be passing through later today. Good choice, Laura." Laura flushes. "This Boru fellah, whilst extremely young, is already making waves. Incidentally, I found out on the *Data Page* Queen Elizabeth is his descendent."

Meathe takes over Laura's tongue. "Whilesh? Whilst? And your scorch, source from wench, whence cometh your inmorfation, information is the

Data Pageth? Don't mix thyme peeriods. My tongue is strangled. Tangled."

Justin breathes into her ear, "Down, babe." She glares at him, "Babe?!" "Sweetichums." "Sweetichums?" "Sweet pea?" he cajoles. "That's besher," Laura slurs, smiling at him in a goofy way. *Of course, she can never be really angry with me*, he burps happily.

Einstein hiccups.

Justin returns his gaze to Ergo. "Let me make this sclear. We're teenagers who don't drink or 'do' dwugs." There, that's one sentence that almost makes sense. "We're not having any smore meash, meathe." Ergo sighs. "Alright. I was aiming for historical accuracy. Apparently, everyone in this period drank the stuff. Sorry."

"Thank you," Justin inclines his head. "We need to be on our little toes."

"On our little toes," Ergo repeats, filing it away.

They walk into the forest and disperse to nap. Gentle snores counter the chatter of squirrels and bird song, Ergo the only one of the group awake.

A couple hours pass before bagpipes are heard in the distance. Ergo pads around, toeing the sleeping forms roughly. Why should she still smart from Justin's rebuff? Because he has her respect, but that doesn't mean she has to take it out on them. She reins in her feelings.

They straggle out of the woods to behold an approaching troop of horsemen and foot soldiers. At the head is a lad seated easily upon a magnificent black destrier. Horse and rider are armored though the young man's red head is bare. Despite his youth, he has a commanding air. Fierce proud warriors fan around behind him, keeping a stately pace.

Laura stumbles against Justin. "A legend in the making," she whispers. "Aye," he says, breaking her spell. "Aye?" "Aye, and he's way too young for you." She smiles, "Jealous?" "Aye, if he were older," he responds. "You have nothing to be jealous of," she bats her eyes in an exaggerated way. He laughs and shoots back the classic movie line, "I know." She elbows him, "I know…two."

The people show loving obeisance to a smiling Boru as he and his escort stop to join in the revelry. The time travelers, forgetting they are invisible to the assembly, also bow.

Laura communicates what she knows of Borus. "It is thought he was born in 926 or perhaps not till 941, though there is speculation he was as old as 88 when he died.

"He attended school in a monastery, studying music, mathematics and language, but his favorite subject was history. He was an avid reader and devoured war stories and studied European military leaders Julius Caesar and Charlemagne to learn their battle tactics. He was discouraged in his military interest so in concession substituted wood weapons to train. When he was sixteen his brother Mathgamain determined it was time for Brian to join him in forcing the Vikings out of Ireland. Boru led guerilla skirmishes against the foe, prevailing against a much larger force, and became one of the greatest Irish generals of all time.

"His parents had been killed by Vikings. When he ousted the Vikings and discovered large numbers of enslaved Irish children in Limerick, he executed 3000 of the enemy.

"Upon his brother's death by Norse treachery in 976, he became King of Tuadmumu, then King of Munster in 978 (to 1014), and finally the last High King of Ireland from 1002-1014. By way of explanation, there were some 150 kings with one High King.

"A visionary, he restored monasteries and libraries throughout the land. Nonetheless, there was much political intrigue and tribal jockeying and he was killed in battle at Clontarf in the year 1014."

Mythril's eyes are like saucers. "Whew! All this because you heard *Brian Boru's March*!"

"Crazy, huh?" says Laura.

"One thing stands out for me. He was 73 or much older, possibly 88, when he died, which is pretty amazing for the time." Mythril turns to Ergo,

"Could it be someone from the future helped with sanitation, especially on the battlefields?"

Ergo stands on her hind legs to clap her wee paws. "Yep, this is in reality your first assignment."

A collective gasp.

"How shall we go about it?" asks Justin.

Ergo, "Hmm, let me dwell upon the question."

Einstein, heretofore silent, "May I address the problem? This calls for a great deal of finesse. Let me see, there is bound to be music and dancing this evening. If I may have use of your abilities, we could perhaps weave the suggestion into the music?"

"Excellent." Ergo and Einstein huddle in vigorous discussion.

****

The musicians tune up as the villagers gather around on the green. Wolf leans in to Mythril, his breath brushing her ear. "The small harp is called a cruit, the fife a feadan and the bagpipe, cuisienna. She turns to him, her lips caressing his cheek, smiling impishly. "Oh." He shivers.

People dance to several lively folk pieces before the minstrels begin a haunting melody that somehow evokes water cupped in…fingers! running several times over…fingers! with soap! Nearly somnambulant, Brian Borus suddenly sits up and cocks his head as though listening to an inner message - turns to the man at his right and orders, "Find soap! Lots of it."

"Soap??!" the man gapes. Brian responds, "I have the strangest gut feeling.". Einstein sits behind him looking pleased.

Ergo beckons it's time to go. Laura takes a final look at the Irish hero.

Chapter Eleven

As they settle into Oisin, Ergo explains that Boru will attribute the mind suggestion about the importance of rigorously washing hands and sterilizing medical instruments to the exhortation of a singing angel. Everyone applauds a blushing Einstein before he huddles to ask Oisin about the magical, repeat magical, technology of time travel. Laura listens but understands nothing though Mythril is…entranced! Turnabout? Ha, ha.

It's a dark night, only a slivered moon and a few stars peeking through the clouds to illuminate Stonehenge. Standing amongst the colossal boulders, wondering how they came to be placed there so long ago, gives everyone goosebumps.

Ergo beckons Wolf near. "Listen." His body becomes fixed. As one, the group stills, time on pause.

They hear a low rumble. Wolf strains forward. Moments pass before his brow clears and he begins to chant in a language unfamiliar to them. They stare in amazement, hardly able to breathe.

The rumbling changes from hoarse to a smoother roughness. They glance around the giant stones, wondering from where the voices come.

An hour passes, Wolf in a trance-like state alternating between chanting and listening, ear cocked. Mythril stands by him. Finally, he emerges from his conversation and turns to grab her, elation on his face.

He turns to the group. "Stonehenge," he explains, "gradually came to life over centuries of occupying a sacred place. They have no recollection how they came to be placed here; it is as baffling to them as to us. They have a deep faith in the earth, the firmament, the elements, all life."

"They?" Laura asks.

Wolf sweeps his arm to encompass the stones. "Yes. They are individuals but also one entity."

"What is the language you used to speak or chant?" Justin enquires.

"Sanskrit. It was difficult at first to understand them. Their voices were hoarse from little use. You must listen carefully to draw them forth." He acknowledges Ergo with a nod. "Tourists hardly let a minute go by without chattering and busying themselves. And not many know Sanskrit.

"Sanskrit is an ancient language of India attributed to Brahma. It is believed that he passed it on to sages who then, from their celestial homes, sent it to humans. By the time it reached Stonehenge, these majestic beings were sentient and naturally gravitated toward it for the language has a life all its own, being holy." He grins at Laura.

Mythril makes a hmm sound. Wolf sniggers, tugging her earlobe. Her smile doesn't erase her trace of skepticism. She walks over to Einstein. "What do you make of this?"

"I do not believe in a personal god with concerns for the fate and actions of humans. That is naïve. I do not believe in an afterlife, but I am not an atheist. If I may be so bold, I am a religious non-believer. Make of that as you will. As for my political beliefs, my moral guide, I am for equality, a socialist economy. With regard to what we just witnessed, I will first search for a scientific explanation before entertaining any other, shall we say, reason." Einstein's lips quirk. "'Cogito ergo sum.'" Then, "'I know one thing, that I know nothing.'"

Ergo reluctantly says it's time to depart. Justin politely asks if it's okay to take photos. Wolf confers with the stones. "They are happy to oblige," he grins.

Wolf commences dialogue with the giants while Justin concentrates on as many photos as he can get from various positions. Feeling chummy, he pats one of them in friendship. Everyone else has been too stunned to react till they leave, when they self-consciously wave goodbye as Wolf bows adieu. Laura shakes herself. "We'll be back," she tentatively promises in a pseudo Arnold Schwarzenegger voice.

Oisin greets them one by one with his charming brogue. "My lady?" he asks Ergo. "To infinity and beyond. No, back to Einstein's time, then our own." Oisin notices the use of the word *our*.

They're off in a flash, Oisin blinking lights at their new stone friends. In no time, they arrive at the scientist's lab. Mythril embraces Einstein with tears in her eyes. He pats her shoulder. "Now, now, we will most likely meet again here, there, everywhere, anywhere! These are challenging problems. I must first devote some time to this Eis McSquard guy before tackling Stonehenge. To think my time space theory has come to fruition! Future fruition. Whatever." "Oh, gawd, Laura's inserted herself into that brain of yours!"

Laura comes up to him. "We didn't get to see Cronus, you know, the Greek god of time, but will next time," playfully swatting him on the shoulder. He laughs, "Cronus, how very interesting. I hope it won't prove untimely dangerous." He waves to the others and turns excitedly to pat his chalkboard before launching into equations.

Off they go in a zippy way. Whew, talk about powerful, profound, peachy keen!! Jubilant, half-hysterical, laughing, giggling, high-fiving, they break into "Rock me, rock me, do, do me rock me," from the Amadeus movie before they arrive in their fourth dimension, which Mythril describes as the (elusive to perceive) indefinite continued progress of existence and events that occur in apparently irreversible succession from the past through the present to the future. She goes on pensively, "And now we may challenge even its linear aspect!"

Anxious to get back to normalcy, Laura turns to Justin, "Hey, you cute cupcake," before smacking him with a full-blown kiss. "You'd better not turn me into a cupcake," he mumbles with a smile. Mythril scowls at Wolf, "How can words be so powerful as to…" umph, he interrupts her perfectly good objection with his lips.

Oisin chuckles. Ergo rolls her eyes.

Fin/e

About the Author

Jerry LeJeune Ferreira Martinez was born in Plaquemine, Louisiana, in 1944. Her family moved to Oakland, California, when she was two before moving to a small village in northern New Mexico in 1952. It is, perhaps, the diversity of this ethnic background that has led to her perspective of the world and universe.

This childhood village life is chronicled in her memoirs, *Looking Back*.

It was from her Mora High School English teacher, Mrs. Tafoya, that she gleaned grammatical and spelling skills. It was also thrilling to learn to type on a manual typewriter, racing to the ping of the bell a few spaces before the righthand margin, following through with a fling of the carriage to start again at the left of the page. It was to become a partnership, the love of reading and writing.

Jerry has resided in Albuquerque with her husband for most of her adult life. They happily have three children, four grandchildren and one great granddaughter, as well as two extremely admirable sons-in-law - and one very energetic daughter-in-law.

Acknowledgements

First, I'd like to thank my fantastic husband, Joe, for his support and forbearance. Oh, yes, forbearance in being such a good sport when I forgot his birthday and scheduled a critique meeting that Saturday!

I'd like to thank my critics, Anna Griego and Ruth Martinez Nakamura. These two fine ladies and excellent poets were spot-on in their assessment throughout *Tuesday Was Two Days Ago*. A lot of work goes into writing, and good positive critique is invaluable. It's that team spirit in any effort - art, music, theatre, movies, business, science, family - that makes the difference.

We had a blast so it was hardly a grim ordeal.

Gracias to my son, Michael, for his support, critique, and stellar aid in publishing (smile).

Also daughter Mary Ancilla Martinez Taasevigen, for her amazing art and critique, as well as grandson, Forrest, for his critique. Thank you!

So, *besitos* to all my family members and close friends I am delighted to embrace.

portal of collective memory

embedded in lambent sun

soft beauty of the female moon

planets and star diamonds pinned to ink

from *Cosmic Touch* by Jerry Martinez

www.ingramcontent.com/pod-product-compliance
Lightning Source LLC
Chambersburg PA
CBHW020333130626
46549CB00003B/1157